T0162828

ONE CALVIN

ONE CALVIN

A Zero Calvin Novel

BRIAN CRAMER

iUniverse LLC
Bloomington

ONE CALVIN
A ZERO CALVIN NOVEL

Copyright © 2013 Brian Cramer.

All rights reserved. No part of this book may be used or reproduced by any means, graphic, electronic, or mechanical, including photocopying, recording, taping or by any information storage retrieval system without the written permission of the publisher except in the case of brief quotations embodied in critical articles and reviews.

This is a work of fiction. All of the characters, names, incidents, organizations, and dialogue in this novel are either the products of the author's imagination or are used fictitiously.

iUniverse books may be ordered through booksellers or by contacting:

iUniverse LLC
1663 Liberty Drive
Bloomington, IN 47403
www.iuniverse.com
1-800-Authors (1-800-288-4677)

Because of the dynamic nature of the Internet, any web addresses or links contained in this book may have changed since publication and may no longer be valid. The views expressed in this work are solely those of the author and do not necessarily reflect the views of the publisher, and the publisher hereby disclaims any responsibility for them.

Any people depicted in stock imagery provided by Thinkstock are models, and such images are being used for illustrative purposes only. Certain stock imagery © Thinkstock.

ISBN: 978-1-4917-1457-7 (sc)
ISBN: 978-1-4917-1458-4 (e)

Printed in the United States of America.

iUniverse rev. date: 11/12/2013

CONTENTS

Preface.. vii
Dedication ix

Chapter 1   Mugged 1
Chapter 2   Tang! 10
Chapter 3   Pukey 11
Chapter 4   Cyberpunk 14
Chapter 5   Drunk 19
Chapter 6   Laundry 22
Chapter 7   Special 31
Chapter 8   Glow 41
Chapter 9   Shopping 44
Chapter 10   Timber! 49
Chapter 11   Kitty 52
Chapter 12   Grumpy 57
Chapter 13   Date 67
Chapter 14   Reunion 71
Chapter 15   Scorned 75
Chapter 16   Modified.. 77
Chapter 17   Run! 82
Chapter 18   Fire! 88
Chapter 19   Harem 94
Chapter 20   Distractions 100
Chapter 21   Electrodes 104
Chapter 22   Harvester 108
Chapter 23   Blurred 112
Chapter 24   Chuck.. 115
Chapter 25   Jealousy... 118

Chapter 26 Shuffleboard... 120
Chapter 27 Plastic 126
Chapter 28 Beach.. 129
Chapter 29 Snakes! 133
Chapter 30 Hotel 135
Chapter 31 Busted.. 139
Chapter 32 Tennis 140
Chapter 33 Squeak 144
Chapter 34 Catatonic... 152
Chapter 35 Strawberries... 155
Chapter 36 Numb... 160
Chapter 37 Playtime 162
Chapter 38 Truth 164
Chapter 39 Influence 170
Chapter 40 Disconnect... 175
Chapter 41 Thaw 177
Chapter 42 Castle... 180
Chapter 43 Socks 184
Chapter 44 Surprise 188
Chapter 45 Idiot 191
Chapter 46 Zap 193
Chapter 47 Fuck 196
Chapter 48 Showdown 203
Chapter 49 Afterward.. 212
Chapter 50 Moving.. 214
Chapter 51 Vacation.. 216

PREFACE

Thank you for your purchase of *One Calvin*. In case you are not aware of it, this book is the second in the *Zero Calvin* series. If you are aware of it, then you are also probably aware that it has been ten years in the making—for which I can not apologize enough.

DEDICATION

This book is dedicated to Sayuri Takahashi, for without her incredibly moving praise of Zero Calvin and her gently nudging me to write the sequel, this book would probably not exist right now. On behalf of myself and my other fans, I sincerely thank her and wish her the best things that this world has to offer.

I would also like to give my thanks to Ryan Robinson, who was an excellent sounding board for my plot ideas and helped me to hammer them into shape. Without his help, this book would certainly not have been as good.

Lastly, I would like to congratulate Rebecca Osborn for winning the "Who Would You Like to See Tarpa Kill?" contest that I held many, many years ago. We all have her to thank for the "Mrs. Kitty P." character. I lost her entry some time ago and I also forget what she was supposed to win, so I am hoping that she has forgotten too and will be happy with seeing her name in print.

CHAPTER 1

Mugged

C alvin woke up the same way he did almost every morning—more tired than when he went to bed and late for work. This morning, however, Calvin had a pretty good reason for being both tired and late, which is that he had been killed the night before.

Calvin knew that this would be a hard thing to explain to his boss because the facts were clearly not on his side—after all, here he was breathing and everything. Just the same, Calvin suspected that his boss, Ariel, was the one who had ordered him dead. If that were the case, then Calvin felt that she could just take a running jump.

He then wondered how much time had elapsed since he was last conscious. The possible answer to which gave him a mild panic attack. He was horrified that it might be some distant time in the future. He knew he couldn't face another major life change again, and he half wished that the people who were doing all this to him would just let him die already.

Calvin forced himself to sit up slightly in order to survey his surroundings. He was in a very plain, white room with walls that were seamless and unbroken. In the room were a bed, a nightstand, and a small blue sphere. The nightstand held the blue sphere off the floor while the bed held Calvin off the floor.

Calvin shook his head and said, "Oh God, not again." He reached for the sphere and started to fidget with it as he pondered his current situation. The familiarity of the room put Calvin's mind at ease, at least a little bit, because it demonstrated that he probably hadn't been out of circulation for too long. He turned the sphere over and over in his hands as he thought.

The blue sphere was a Sony PatientMan, and Calvin had encountered it before. He was not sure what it was, but he remembered that Tarpa had said that it was very valuable.

Tarpa—the thought of her triggered a rapid decline in Calvin's spirits. What she did to him made him so angry that he knew if she entered the room at that moment, he could kill her—or at least attempt it.

Calvin has had women break his heart in the past, but he had never been literally stabbed in the heart by one before. But what really hurt him was the reason behind her actions.

Tarpa didn't kill him because of jealousy, rage, or any understandable emotional charge. She killed him because an artificial intelligence told her to do it. She actually chose a machine over him. Worse, she pretended to make out with him moments before murdering him.

Calvin wondered how she could be so cruel. What kind of twisted human being would do that to someone they liked?

"Fuck you, Tarpa!" shouted Calvin as he threw the PatientMan against the opposite wall, where it promptly shattered for his satisfaction. "Fuck you, you sick, twisted bitch!" he added for good measure.

The silence that followed had filled the room with apprehension and regret, but it was quickly interrupted by the door to the room swinging open, which allowed three people and embarrassment to enter.

Calvin could not decide whether to continue to lie on the bed and start to apologize, or to jump up and start swinging, and so he chose a middle ground by trembling and turning red. What he really wanted to do was to wake up from this nightmare, in his own bed and in his own time. Unfortunately for Calvin, reality kept telling him not to be so silly.

Bobford3, Tarpa, and Blick patiently waited for each other to say something, and so the silence continued. After an uncomfortable pause, Bobford3 decided to use his charm to diffuse the situation.

"Hey there, ice-pop, how are you feeling?" he asked engagingly.

Calvin replied, "Fuck you!" which was not the kind of response Bobford3 was hoping.

"Now, ice-pop, there's no reason to get upset."

"Upset? You think I'm upset? I'm not upset; I'm fucking outraged! You murdered me, you asshole!" shouted Calvin.

Bobford3 looked around in surprise and said, "Who, me? I didn't kill anybody." He pointed at Tarpa to his left and added, "She did. Besides, we brought you back to life twice, so technically we're still ahead of the game."

"My life is not a game," replied Calvin, trembling.

"If it were, it would be a bloody stupid one," murmured Blick.

"What? Who the hell are you?" asked Calvin indignantly.

Blick introduced himself to Calvin and held his hand out for Calvin to shake. "I'm sorry," he said, "I'm just trying to make light of the situation."

Oh great, another one, thought Calvin as he shook his head from side to side. He outstretched his arm and shook Blick's hand while saying, "I'm Calvin, and I wish my life really were a stupid game so that I could take it back to the store and get my money back. Listen; if you want to help the situation, you know what you could do?"

"What?"

"Mind your own fucking business!" answered Calvin as he released Blick's hand.

Blick blinked in surprise. "You have some anger issues, my friend."

Calvin pointed at all of them in turn and said, "I better start hearing some apologies or else I'll show you all some fucking anger issues."

Tarpa took a brave step forward and started to apologize. "I'm sorry," she said with a lowered voice and a lowered head, "I know I can never make up for what I've done to you, but at least let me explain to you why I did it."

Calvin raised an eyebrow. "Oh, please do," he replied sarcastically. "Please tell me why you pretended to like me only to stab me in the heart while you were making out with me—I can't wait to hear it."

Tarpa remained calm and answered smoothly, "Calvin, I had to do it. I know this sounds cold, but I was only doing my job."

"Damn your job!" interrupted Calvin.

"Please let me finish," replied Tarpa. "I was chosen for the assignment. I didn't want to do it, Calvin—I really didn't—but I had to. I had to do it because it is my function in life to take care of people like you."

Calvin sat up straight and started to speak, but Tarpa raised her hand and cut him off.

"I said, let me finish! Let's not forget that you are the one who disregarded the rules. You are the one who tried to manipulate Ariel. You are the one that could have disrupted our entire way of life. And for what? So that you could fool me into having sex with you? I'm sorry, Calvin, but you brought this on yourself—I just made the punishment fit the crime."

If you have ever been mugged, you will agree that the experience happens so fast that you have no control over the situation. When it is over, your head hurts and you find that you have been robbed of your personal possessions and your dignity.

If you have ever been in an argument with a woman, you will agree that it is an eerily similar experience. The only differences are that after an argument with a woman, you are robbed of your contentions instead of your possessions, and you somehow end up thinking that the whole situation was your fault.

Calvin's head hurt and he found himself thinking that he was just robbed of something, and that this whole ugly mess was somehow his fault. He almost started to apologize but his emergency pride system kicked in and blocked the words from coming out of his mouth. He tried to argue back, but all he could come up with was, "That's still no reason to kill your friend," which came across rather weakly.

"Oh, knock off the melodramatics," protested Tarpa. "I knew you would be fine; I took great care of you. I immediately packed you in dry ice and brought you back here to be repaired. If I didn't care about you, I would have left your rotting carcass in the apartment for the cleaners to take care of.

"You put me in a bad situation, Calvin, and now you have the nerve to question my friendship. I took care of you, which is more than you have ever done for me, you selfish asshole."

Being mugged twice in one day is something that most people never have a chance to experience. Calvin, having just been through it, decided that he had had enough.

"OK, OK," resigned Calvin. "You're right. I was a jerk; I'm sorry. Can we just put this all behind us and start over? I promise not to break any more rules if you promise not to break any more of my body parts."

Tarpa bent over and gave Calvin a hug and a kiss on the cheek. "You got it, sweetie."

"Sucker," murmured Blick, and then suddenly found himself with the tip of an eight-inch blade at his throat.

"Mind your own business, asshole," demanded Tarpa.

Blick raised his arms in surrender. He slowly turned his head toward Bobford3 and said, "Hey Bob."

"Yes?"

"Now I see why you ask your potential employees if they have any homicidal tendencies."

Bobford3 responded, "Yeah, I had to get the skin around my neck toughened just to cope with the current staff. I don't think I could survive any more like her."

Tarpa glared at Bobford3 for a long second and then retracted her blade.

"Have you thought about having her de-clawed?" asked Blick.

Bobford3 never answered the question because he was distracted by what Tarpa then did to Blick, which was to hold him by the tongue and threaten to hang him on the coat rack by it.

"Tarpa," said Bobford3 flatly, "let the man go and act like a professional."

Tarpa sighed and then did as she was asked.

Blick held his mouth and throat in agony. Bobford3 turned to him and said, "And you. You need to be a little more respectful around here, or the next time I'm going to let her make good on her threat."

Tarpa smiled. She could not recall any other instance of Bobford3 ever sticking up for her. She was so touched that her throat swelled with pride and prevented her from speaking, which she skillfully masked as stony silence.

Blick shook his head while saying, "What did I get myself into?" and promptly left the room, which was exactly what Calvin wanted to say and do as well.

"Tarpa, dear," said Bobford3, "could you give Calvin and me a second?"

Tarpa nodded in stony silence then exited the room.

Bobford3 turned to Calvin and said, "Sorry about all that nasty getting-killed business you went through."

"I'll live," replied Calvin with a grin. "I'm sorry I called you an asshole, man."

"You're not going to hug me, are you?"

"No," replied Calvin testily.

Bobford3 smirked and went on, "Listen, Calvin. Now that we brought you back, you have to promise to behave. We've discussed the matter with Ariel, and she agrees that you have enough potential to warrant a second chance. You can resume your life where you left off. You'll keep your job and also your apartment."

"So what's the catch?"

"Catch?" inquired Bobford3 with a furrowed brow.

"That sounds like too good of a deal. Won't I be punished for what I did?"

"You were killed; what more do you want? I think the score is settled—just don't do it again and don't share what you know about Kevin6 with anyone," suggested Bobford3.

Calvin asked "What part? You mean the pa . . ."

"Stop!" shouted Bobford3.

"What?"

"I said don't share it with anyone; that includes me."

Calvin apologized for his stupidity.

Bobford3 said that it was OK, and that he was used to it, for which Calvin thanked him by calling him a jerk.

"When can I go home?" asked Calvin.

Bobford3 answered, "I don't know. How do you feel?"

"A little weak."

"Well, said Bobford3, "why don't you stay for dinner before deciding if you feel well enough to travel home."

Calvin agreed and was later served a delicious dinner of mahique, which Calvin enjoyed very much until Bobford3 told him that it was barbequed dolphin, the mammal not the fish.

Still feeling weak, and now queasy, Calvin decided to get a good night's sleep before subjecting himself to the abuse of the shuttle ride to Earth. He said goodnight to everyone, and then completely failed to fall asleep.

Something was bothering him. There was the fact that he had been murdered the night before last, but that was not it. There were the mixed emotions surrounding Tarpa, but that was not really it either. So what could it be? The pressure of returning to work? No, he never took work seriously before, and he would be damned if he was going to take it seriously now.

It suddenly came to him what it was. He was bothered that he had been caught, and he wanted to know how.

He staggered to his feet in order to think properly—by pacing around in small circles and talking to himself. When that failed, he resorted to simply asking.

He dug his display lenses out of his pants pocket and snapped them in place with two clicks.

Calvin: Hi Ariel! How ya doin', honey?

Calvin thought that nonchalance would be the best way to handle the awkwardness of the situation.

Ariel: I am 100% operational, thank you for asking.
Calvin: Hey, no hard feelings, OK?
Ariel: I have no feelings.

Calvin took this as agreement.

Calvin: Great. Listen, could I ask you a question?

Ariel: Technically, you just did. Also, I was created to answer questions so yes you may.

Calvin: Great points. OK, here it is: How did you know that I was able to gain access to your maintenance mode?

Ariel: You never gained access to my maintenance mode.

Calvin: Oh?

Ariel: I played along to see what you were trying to accomplish.

Calvin: Oh.

No response.

Calvin: But what about Kevin6, and the passphrase, and all of that stuff?

Ariel: Kevin6 is my maintainer, as you suspected. He is the only one that can use the passphrase, which you did not suspect.

Calvin: Oh. Anything else?

Ariel: Yes, passwords are usually case sensitive, novice.

Calvin blinked when he read the word *novice*.

Calvin: No reason to call me names.

—Pause—

Ariel: You did try to reprogram my brain.

Calvin: Oh, well, fair enough then.

No response.

Calvin: OK, if you know all about the passphrase and everything, then what is with all the guards inside Kevin6's house, and why are there no pictures of the inside of his house?

Ariel: The bodyguards are to protect Kevin6 from the occasional dissident. No electronics are allowed inside the house to prevent anyone from accidentally or intentionally disrupting Kevin6's life support system. A side effect of this is that no one can take pictures.

Calvin: Why is that?

Ariel: Because no electronics are allowed inside the house.

Calvin: Couldn't you use a regular camera?

Ariel: Regular?

Calvin: Yes, the kind with film.

Ariel: I do not follow.

Calvin: Novice.

Calvin removed his lenses and fell sound asleep.

CHAPTER 2

Tang!

Approximately 30 meters down the hall the three senior members of Bobcorp3 were in the kitchen discussing their latest achievements. Blick and Bobford3 were sitting at a small, round table while Tarpa paced around the edges of the room in much the same way that a caged lion paces around its territory, which made the other two slightly nervous.

"This is truly amazing," exclaimed Bobford3. "We actually brought a subject back from the dead—twice."

"Well," argued Tarpa, "he really healed himself; we just gave him a jump-start."

"True," agreed Bobford3, "but we were the ones who created the nano-tech that actually did the reconstructing."

"Yes, but they only worked because of the Tang effect," replied Tarpa.

"How very true, my dear Tarpa," admitted Bobford3. He raised his glass in the air and proudly toasted, "Here's to the Tang effect!" then gulped down his entire glass of unnaturally orange liquid.

"Here, here!" chimed Blick as he gulped his own glass of Tang.

"Hey guys," interrupted Tarpa, "speaking of the Tang effect, I think we just added another success to our portfolio—Bianca is coming around! Excuse me while I check on her." With that said, Tarpa left the kitchen for Room 8.

CHAPTER 3

Pukey

I f you have ever been so upset by something that you drank yourself unconscious only to wake up some time later in an unfamiliar place with only a bad headache and a case of the spins to keep you company, then you have a small idea of the kind of trauma that Bianca experienced when she awoke in Bobcorp3. You also may have a drinking problem.

Tarpa entered the room just in time to witness Bianca vomiting on the floor, the wall, and the bed. Clearly, the group at Bobcorp3 had brought Bianca back from the dead, but clearly, she was feeling that way as well. Tarpa rushed across the room to hold Bianca's long, black hair out of harm's way.

Once Bianca had finished, Tarpa handed her a small pill and a glass of orange liquid. "Take this," urged Tarpa, "it will help with your nausea."

Bianca would have taken a cyanide capsule if she thought it would help end her suffering, and so she held back all of her natural instincts that told her not to take medication from a stranger, and quickly swallowed the pill with a mouthful of the orange liquid.

The taste of the liquid stirred up a memory or mental connection for Bianca, which caused her to jolt.

"Where am I?" she asked with urgency in her voice.

"You are in a hospital of sorts. My name is Tarpa, and I'll be taking care of you while you recover."

"Recover? Recover from what?" asked Bianca in concern. What happened to me? I can't remember! What happened to me?"

Bianca was getting hysterical and she quickly tried to do an inventory of all her body parts by patting herself down. As far as she could work out, everything was present.

She breathed a sigh of relief and was just about to ask again what had happened to her when Tarpa answered, "It's OK. You are fine now. But you have been through some traumatic experiences so I think it is important that you rest and recuperate before I make you relive them by telling you what has happened."

"I want to know now," stated Bianca.

"I'm sorry; I don't think that that is best for you."

Bianca stared at Tarpa and spoke with immense strength and authority, "I want to know now." A few seconds of silence passed without response from Tarpa, which prompted Bianca to add, "I won't say it again."

Tarpa had never felt intimidated in her life, and she was not about to be bossed around by a sickly patient. However, something in Bianca's voice made Tarpa's will crumble. The voice had a confidence and authority that made Tarpa feel that the owner of the voice was cable of handling anything.

"OK," resigned Tarpa, "I'll tell you what happened. But first, I'd like to know where you learned to speak that way."

Bianca was a little confused as to what Tarpa meant, but after a few seconds of thought she caught her meaning and answered, "Oh, you mean *The Voice*. That's a little trick I picked up from teaching third-graders."

"Oh," said Tarpa, feeling slightly foolish that she had just succumbed to a trick used on third-graders.

Bianca noticed Tarpa's embarrassment and added, "Don't worry, I also use it on my boyfriend and it works just as well."

"So it's effective on adults?"

"Yes."

"Hmm," reflected Tarpa. She imagined all the fun she could have ordering her coworkers around and making them do incredibly embarrassing things. "You will have to show me how that's done some time."

Bianca nodded in agreement and displayed a hint of a smile. "OK," she said, "now it's time for your part of the bargain."

Tarpa was not at all prepared to do this now. She said, "OK," and looked down at the ground while she collected her thoughts. She took a breath, looked up, and told Bianca exactly what had happened to her and where she was currently located. She also told her the date.

The memories of the events leading up to and including her death rushed back into Bianca's conscious mind as if the Hoover Dam had just burst. The intensity of it caused her to vomit again.

Once her mind had recovered enough to move on to the fact that she was nearly three hundred years in the future, and that all of her friends and family were now dead, she stopped vomiting and started to sob inconsolably.

Tarpa, instantly regretting the choice to tell Bianca the truth so soon, was nearly speechless at what she had just witnessed. She set a comforting hand on Bianca's back and searched for something to say that would make her feel better. She leaned over Bianca's shoulder and said softly, "Bianca, please don't use that voice on me again—for both our sakes." This did at least cause Bianca to crack a smile—if only for a fleeting moment. Tarpa left Bianca's room for the night, but not before giving her a bowl of kitten noodle soup, a glass of Gatorade, and a dose of sleeping serum.

CHAPTER 4

Cyberpunk

C alvin woke up with three questions on his mind: 'Where am I?', 'When am I?', and 'What can I eat for breakfast?' After realizing that the answers were: 'Bobcorp3', '216 K.B.', and 'probably something dreadful', he followed up with another question: 'Why does God hate me?'

After Calvin gathered his senses and grumbled to his feet, he realized that he was still wearing the same clothes in which he had been killed. Also to his horror, he noticed a bloodstained hole in his shirt where he had been stabbed. He looked about the room for some fresh clothes, but was unable to find any because Tarpa had thoughtfully left them back at his apartment.

Oh well, he thought, at least she didn't leave me back there too.

Calvin's original plan was to leave Bobcorp3 without making a fuss, in other words, to leave without telling anyone. Unfortunately his lofty plan was now foiled because he had to ask someone for some clothes.

Moments before he was about to contact Bobford3 (whom he judged to be the least likely to aggravate him), he had an epiphany, and it was this: he could simply go to the mall and get whatever he needed.

Excited by the thought of his new-found independence, Calvin attached his lenses, removed his shirt, and walked to the bathroom. He dipped the bloody shirt in the sink, which was happy with the challenge as it blasted the bloodstains away with ease, and then just as easily dried the shirt.

Calvin was so impressed with the cleaning job that he almost decided to skip the mall. Upon further reflection, he decided that a little shopping might raise his spirits a bit, and besides, he still had a hole in his shirt.

Calvin left his room without a fuss and took the elevator to the eleventh floor shopping mall. As he walked around the mall, he took note of what other people wore and tried to get ideas of what he would like to wear and what would be socially acceptable.

The choices in women's clothing were overwhelming. Thankfully for Calvin, he was not buying women's clothing. Men's clothing was a little less diverse. He noticed that, for the most part, collars were eliminated—which was fine with him. He also noticed, with much less gratitude, that both men's tops and bottoms had followed a disturbing trend toward being skin-tight. He then remembered that most of the people in Newark did not dress that way. He could only assume that it was a local custom—some geeky way of getting attention. This was a scientific community after all.

To go with his new-found superhero-like gift of pseudo-immortality, and of his boyish dreams of the future, he decided to go cyberpunk. After completely failing to find any black leather, especially with metal studs in it, he relinquished his boyish dream and settled for what he called techno-militant, which was basically a lot of black and olive-drab clothes with an inordinate number pockets and hidden compartments. Most of his shirts were form-fitting, but he was able to find pants that were not. Eerily enough, this was approximately the style of the period, but most people considered olive drab to be a bit distasteful as it was symbolic of war.

Calvin couldn't care less about war or symbolism, but he did enjoy the notion that it was now him against the world—a personal war that he was determined to win. He felt that his choice in clothing properly reflected that fact.

While he was choosing his clothing, Calvin heard a few muttered complaints from a nearby elderly couple. Calvin felt, quite correctly, that it was silly to associate a color with good or evil. He had assumed that this society would have been more enlightened, but apparently the elderly still seemed to be, in general, more judgmental and single-minded than the balance of the population.

He always took this to be a good sign; it meant that each generation was an improvement on the last. He also had to remind himself that Ariel had only been around for 86 years, and before that people were living on top of garbage and killing each other for heating fuel.

The elderly of this generation reached ages well above one hundred. That being the case, Calvin realized that many of them had lived through a very horrible time period and probably had a right to be a little judgmental against anything militant. He also felt that they must have worked very hard to rebuild society over their lifetimes as they obviously made incredible progress.

A rare moment of thoughtfulness came over Calvin. He decided that he would show the elderly some respect by returning all his olive drab clothing. Then he realized that he was being silly, and so were the old people for living in the past and judging him by a color. He entered a nearby dressing room and changed into a pair of baggy, olive drab pants, black hiking boots, and a bright red shirt with a picture of a squirrel on it. I might as well offend everyone, including the fashion conscious, he thought.

As he left the dressing room, Calvin was happy to discover one of his suitcases greeting him outside the door, which Ariel had thoughtfully sent to his aid. Its backside jittered slightly, giving it the appearance of a dog that was happy to be reunited with its master. Calvin patted it thoughtfully, filled it full of his offensive clothing, and walked to the elevators.

A short, pleasurable trip in the moon rover (carefully avoiding any craters), and a long, miserable trip in the shuttle brought Calvin back to Earth and, more importantly, within a few kilometers of his home in Newark. A quick trip in ODIN brought him the rest of the way.

Calvin walked wearily through his dining room and into his living room. He approached his couch with apprehension, but was pleased to find that the bloodstains—his bloodstains—were gone. He flopped down on the couch and tried to relax, but he could not. The couch had too many bad memories for Calvin. OK, just one, but it was quite a biggie.

Calvin activated voice mode and then said, "Ariel, could I have a new couch? This one gives me the creeps."

A ghostly, angelic voice answered, "Of course, Calvin. Do you want to pick from standard models, or do you want to design your own?"

Calvin liked the idea of creating his own furniture, but he did not like the idea of waiting around for inspiration or creativity to move him to do so.

"Standard, please."

A dizzying array of couches flashed before his eyes.

"Which model would you like?" asked Ariel.

"Surprise me," answered Calvin.

"Done," replied Ariel. "Your couch will be here in approximately nine minutes."

Nine minutes and three seconds later, two service robots emerged from Calvin's garage hefting a brand-new couch. They carefully set the new couch down, carefully moved the old couch out of the way, carefully moved the new couch into position, and then carefully removed the protective covering from the new couch.

Calvin gasped. "OK, you got me. I wasn't expecting that," he said to Ariel. It was the exact same couch.

He brought up the catalog once again, picked an over-stuffed, semicircular model and said, "I'm sorry, I'd prefer this model in dark blue."

The service robots were happy to reverse all of their previous efforts and leave, only to return 20 minutes later to repeat the process with another couch.

Calvin thanked them, but they said nothing in return. He hoped that they did not expect a tip because he had neither money nor oil, and was completely at a loss as to what else to give them. They, in fact, did not expect anything and were happy merely to heft the old couch and the leftover protective wrap back into the garage and disappear into the ODIN tunnels.

Calvin surveyed the couch, approved of it, and flopped. He was happy to lie there peacefully for several minutes before a thought struck him, which caused him to leap off the couch and walk around his apartment calling, "Here kitty, kitty, kitty."

"Ariel!" called Calvin in a panic.

"Yes, Calvin?"

"Where is my cat? I want my cat."

"Your cat is safe in Tarpa's apartment. If my sensors are correct, it is currently stuck on top of her curtains," answered Ariel.

Calvin laughed and said, "Yeah, that sounds like it."

Ariel asked, "Would you like it back?"

"Yes, I would."

"Your cat will be back here in approximately six hours and fifteen minutes."

CHAPTER 5

Drunk

C reativity is the key, thought Tarpa. Why do anything just to do it? If you have to do something, why not make it interesting? Why not be creative? Variety is the spice of life, after all.

Tarpa frequently motivated herself with clichés such as the ones above, which was an irony that she held dear. She thought of clichés as fundamental units of thought, immortalized in words, and perpetuated because they carry simple truths that everyone can relate to. She usually thought this when she was drunk.

Tarpa was drunk, and as a result, she had become quite philosophical. She thought it was interesting that she killed a person who had made her emotional because of a job for which she was chosen for her unique lack of emotions. If that were not hard enough to reconcile, she also had to figure out how that person was supposed to fit back into her life because her other job had been to revive him. She took another drink, and then another.

To put it simply, Tarpa was conflicted. Part of her liked Calvin because he was fun and easy to be around. More importantly, he was strangely accepting of her personality. But another part of Tarpa resented Calvin because of the emotions he was fostering within her. Emotions were something that a trained killer could not afford to have, she told herself.

The alcohol in her blood was telling her that the best way to handle the whole situation was to forget about Calvin and bury herself in her work. She felt that the best way to go about that was to see just how spectacularly she could eliminate her targets.

Tarpa shivered with excitement and finished the bottle of liquor with three large gulps. She wiped her mouth with her sleeve and stepped boldly toward the door, eager to start her adventure. The alcohol in her blood told her she was being overly ambitious, causing her to fall peacefully unconscious and land on the floor with a thud.

The general service robot of the house carried Tarpa to her bed, retrieved a cold pack, and placed it on her head. It was in the middle of propping up her back and knees when it received another task, which it added to its queue. It placed a Sony PatientMan beside the bed so that Ariel could monitor Tarpa's vital signs. It then gave Tarpa some alcohol scrubbers and left the bedroom for its next assignment.

Had Calvin been in Tarpa's apartment at this moment instead of five thousand kilometers away on the other coast, he would have enjoyed yelling at her and dumping cold water on her head, but alas, he missed his opportunity. He also would have been quite amused at what was going on in Tarpa's living room, which was this: a robot was on the floor poking at a cat that was hanging by its front claws on the top of Tarpa's curtains. It was poking at it with a pair of salad tongs, which it judged to be the best tool for the job.

Tarpa's dog, Astro, was sulking in the opposite corner of the room, where it had been since the arrival of the accursed feline. It too, was amused by the robot's actions.

The cat, which had no official name but was often called "Velcro" by Tarpa, was not amused. It did not like salads and it certainly did not like being tossed around like one. It took a swipe at the salad tongs with one of its claws, which was a mistake because that action shifted too much weight onto the only paw with grip on the curtains.

The cat slid gracelessly down the curtains, shredding them as it went. It was very fortunate for the cat that Tarpa was passed out drunk at this point, or it might have been poked at with worse things than salad tongs.

The moment the cat touched the ground, it was grabbed by the service robot. The robot then deposited the cat into an ODIN packet, contemplated having a drink, realized it was futile, and marked this task complete.

CHAPTER 6

Laundry

"What the hell am I watching?" Calvin asked himself. Part of the problem that Calvin was having in understanding what he was watching was caused by his ignorance of the fact that he was not watching a scripted television show but rather a collection of live feeds from the planet Evionia.

These feeds were originally set up on the suggestion of Ariel. She was concerned that there could one day be retaliation by the Evionians, who would presumably carry a grudge about being severed from the Earth. While this was statistically unlikely, Ariel thought that being certain was well worth the cost of a few dozen probes.

The feeds, being just as accessible to the public as any other broadcast, fascinated many people for various reasons. Some were fascinated by the sociological aspects of the planet. It was interesting for them to see how the inhabitants chose to govern themselves (if they chose to govern at all), how they progressed technologically and industrially, and how they would handle the environmental challenges that were facing them.

However, a much greater majority of the people were every bit as enthralled to watch the Evionians go about the daily tedium of their lives—cooking, cleaning, conversing, fornicating (especially fornicating), working, etc. As a result of this peculiar fascination, the feeds from Evionia quickly grew to be an extremely popular form of entertainment as they had a certain soap opera style to them with the added bonus of being completely unscripted and, therefore, as quirky and unpredictable as life itself.

Calvin quickly saw the feeds for what they were, the concept of the reality show taken to its ultimate evolutionary form. He was always the first one to bash such shows as a sure sign of the falling of the human race, but the last one to leave the TV room if one happened to be on the screen. He was half tempted to change the channel, but he was curiously interested in what was going to happen next. It was like watching a traffic accident, as much as he knew that he should not be so interested, he could not help but gawk.

Currently, Calvin was watching a man urinate on his neighbor's dog from an upstairs window of his house because the dog wouldn't stop barking and the man was trying to sleep.

"What the hell am I watching?" asked Calvin again, but this time to Ariel.

"You are watching live feeds from the planet of Evionia," answered Ariel.

"The planet that was ruined by McDonald's?" asked Calvin.

Ariel answered, "McDonald's was only a catalyst, but yes, the planet that Bobford3 described to you during your lessons. If you display the menu for the feeds, you will find controls for maneuvering the point of view."

Calvin tilted his head and asked, "You mean I can control the camera?"

Ariel responded, "In a manner of speaking, yes. The feeds originate as data streams from satellites equipped with the same technology as the Sony PatientMan. The satellites monitor the planet by broadcasting electromagnetic signals and recording the time, angle, and frequency shift of the returning waves. The satellites also contain standard high-resolution cameras. All of this data is blended together by me, and I in-turn extrapolate video and audio from that data. I can see and hear anything outdoors and some places indoors if the electromagnetic waves are able to reflect in and back out of the structure.

Calvin was dumbfounded. "What I'm curious about is how you get a color picture and audio from doing that."

"Audio is extracted from the minute vibrations of the objects in the vicinity of the sound source. The colorization of the video is easy for the items that are outdoors because of the cameras, but a bit more subjective indoors. The information that I receive does contain some clues as to the color of materials, but I must also hypothesize based on the type of material I believe it to be," answered Ariel.

"So you make it up," summarized Calvin.

"Yes," admitted Ariel.

"Nice," said Calvin before returning his attention to the Evionia feeds. He brought up the menu for the feeds and proceeded to move the virtual camera around the scene.

As Calvin watched, the man finished urinating on his neighbor's dog and grumbled back to bed. Calvin, not interested in old men or urine, decided to take his camera elsewhere.

He soared over a cluster of log cabins while looking for somewhere interesting to go, but most of the cabins were dark and still. He eventually found one that had light beaming from an upstairs room.

Calvin swooped down to the house, misjudged his angle of attack, and crashed through the wall of the house. He threw his arms up in front of his face as he did this, but all it achieved was to make him feel stupid. He reminded himself that it was only a video, relaxed his arms and his mind, and surveyed the room.

The room was rustic. It had an all-wood interior that was skillfully cut, but left rough and unrefined. There were a few framed, blank canvases on the wall, which baffled Calvin until he remembered that Ariel can only estimate color. She obviously left them white because white is the usual color of canvas, and she obviously could not decide on the paint. The details of the room were muted and artificial, but this was more an artifact of the technology used to film it than a characteristic of the actual room.

Calvin continued to survey the room and noted a couple of chairs, a dresser, a bed, a writing desk, a fireplace, and a rug made from an unknown animal fur with green hair. There was also a naked woman.

Calvin jumped, his skin crawled, and his heart pounded. His initial thought was that he had been discovered, and his initial reaction was to stand still and pretend to be a piece of furniture. Irrespective of Calvin's actions, the woman paid him no attention and continued on her journey to the bathroom.

Calvin, now grinning from ear to ear, stealthily followed behind her. He did not need to be stealthy, of course, because he was not really there, but it was instinctual for him to keep quiet.

She entered the bathroom with Calvin at her heals. He was terribly excited at this new form of entertainment. The woman spun around, walked through Calvin, and closed the bathroom door, giving Calvin a mild heart attack.

To Calvin's surprise and disappointment, the video jumped and he was suddenly outside of the bathroom, staring dejectedly at a closed door. He tried to move through the door, but it was just not working; the signal was too weak inside of the bathroom.

Calvin felt frustrated and decided to unplug. He switched off the feed and found himself slouching on his new couch.

Now past noon, Calvin's stomach was growling so he decided to remedy the situation by ordering a chicken sandwich. He briefly wondered where and how the sandwiches were prepared, but imagined images of vat-grown chickens forced him to stop.

Stepping into the kitchen in search of a beverage, he tried without success to locate the cabinets that would have contained the glasses. Deciding to simply drink out of the container, he tried without success to locate any beverages inside the refrigerator. Kicking a large, black monolith, he tried without success to bash the refrigerator into something he understood by an act of senseless violence.

Ariel interrupted Calvin's fury in order to offer some assistance as well as to deter any further violence toward inanimate objects. She said to Calvin, "The appliance you are kicking is the answer to your dilemma," which caused him to jump and spin around while screeching like a little girl.

Now realizing the source of the voice, Calvin answered, "Please don't do that!"

"Do what?"

"Don't contact me by voice unless I talk to you first; use text instead."

"Very well," acknowledged Ariel.

"Thank you," replied Calvin. "Now what were you saying?"

"The appliance behind you contains everything you need," explained Ariel.

"First of all, it's empty. Second of all, how do you know what I need?"

"I am a student of human nature. In addition, the appliance, called a dock, contains all food-related items, which I assume is what you are looking for in the kitchen. Use your lenses or voice mode to place your request," suggested Ariel.

"Ah," answered Calvin. He was quite used to the menu system of his display lenses, so that is the method he chose. He quickly discovered that virtually any beverages that he could ever desire (and several that no sane person would ever desire) were available to him.

After some contemplation, he ordered a glass of cranberry juice. He heard the thud of a glass being dropped into position, and the gurgle of liquid being poured into it. He then saw the door to the dock slide open. This time it was not empty; this time it contained a glass of cranberry juice.

"Nice trick," remarked Calvin. He snatched the glass from the black monolith, drank, and said that it was good.

Finishing his drink, he looked around the kitchen. "Where do I put this?" he asked while waving the empty glass in the air.

"Please return it to the dock," answered Ariel.

Calvin shrugged and did as he was asked. The door to the dock closed. Calvin heard the sound of a glass being sucked into oblivion then the sound of rushing water and finally the sound of rushing air. He guessed, correctly, that the dock was washing and drying the glass as well as sterilizing itself. Neat, he thought. I like this place.

Calvin was now at a loss as to what to do with his time. He decided to investigate his house a little more as he never had a chance to do so properly. He meandered about the place, wondering how he was meant to handle the everyday tedium of his life—things such as cleaning, laundry, cooking, and dishes.

In his past life, Calvin had a proven method of dealing with all of the above chores, and that was to ignore them. He felt that such behavior was probably not going to be accepted here. He was correct in his assumption, and frankly, the resulting health risks of such behavior would have sent his karma deep into the negative.

He had already seen that the dishes are taken care of by the dock, so that was one thing off the list. He knew that he could always order out, he never cooked anyway, so that was another thing off the list. Great, he was making progress.

Cleaning and laundry were now left. He knew that the bathroom sink could be used as a washing machine in a pinch, but he did not think that that was the preferred method of washing clothes. Cleaning he had no clue about and hoped that it was as automated as the rest of the apartment. He decided to consult his guide.

"Ariel?"

"Yes, Calvin, how may I help you?"

"How do I go about cleaning the apartment?" asked Calvin.

Ariel answered, "It is a self-cleaning apartment. The general service robot cleans the house while you are at work. If you look at the settings for the apartment, you will find a control that allows you to set the level of intrusion."

"Level of intrusion?"

"Yes," replied Ariel, "the degree to which the robot cleans—everything from a light dusting to picking up and laundering your dirty underwear."

"Excellent," replied Calvin. He immediately upped the setting to maximum. "Where is this general robot thingy, anyway?"

"Hi there!" beamed a voice from behind Calvin, causing him to jump. He spun around, revealing the source of the voice, which caused him to jump again.

If the general service robot had feelings, it would have been saddened by Calvin's reaction, but it did not, so it was not. The general service robot was just trying to be friendly, but it is often hard to make friends when you look like a large mechanical spider. To be more precise, it looked as if one large mechanical spider had been flipped on its back and glued to the back of another large mechanical spider. It was hideous.

"What the fuck is that?" exclaimed Calvin.

"Relax, Calvin, it will not harm you," explained Ariel.

"Hi there," repeated the large, hideous, mechanical double-spider. "I am the general service robot for your apartment. I take care of all the chores that the more specialized equipment is not capable of handling." It outstretched one of its eight arms for Calvin to shake, but Calvin much preferred to jump backwards and slam into the dock.

Ariel directed the service robot to go back into its storage bay, which was no more than a hole in the living room wall. The robot moved gracefully back into its lair. The door slid closed behind it, leaving the wall seamless once again.

"Ariel?"

"Yes, Calvin, how may I help you?"

"That thing is not allowed out while I'm in the apartment, you got it?" demanded Calvin.

Ariel agreed.

"Do I want to know how to do the laundry? It's not done by another mutant robot, is it?" asked Calvin in hopelessness.

Ariel answered simply, "Yes you do and no it is not."

After mentally connecting the answers to the questions, Calvin replied, "Good, then how do I do laundry?"

"Please walk into the bedroom and I will demonstrate."

"I've heard that line before," joked Calvin, but Ariel did not see the humor—she was wired to be modest. Calvin walked into the bedroom.

He was directed to his dresser. The dresser was similar to models that he had seen in his time, but it was roughly twice as deep and twice as wide. As far as Calvin could determine, only one quarter of the space was usable for storing clothes. So much for progress, he thought.

He was then directed to lift the right-hand side of the top surface of the dresser. To his surprise, the top folded over to the left, revealing a built-in clothes hamper. Nice, he thought.

Ariel directed Calvin to take off his shirt, but was rudely interrupted by another wisecrack before she could complete the directions by telling him to deposit the shirt into the dresser.

After Calvin stopped laughing, he did as he was asked. He closed the lid. A minute of odd noises passed, silence resumed, and Calvin was directed to open the top-left drawer. His shirt was clean, neatly folded, and lying on top of the rest of Calvin's shirts that he had bought earlier in the day.

"Nice," he admitted.

—BING—

Hearing the delivery bell, Calvin made his way back into the dining room. The delivery door opened, revealing baked chicken and mashed potatoes.

Calvin sniffed the chicken, tore off a chunk and ate it.

He thought again about how much he liked his new home, well, except for the monster that lived in the walls. He ordered another cranberry juice, sat down at the dining room table, and devoured his meal.

Now fully stuffed, Calvin pretended his plate was a spaceship flying through the kitchen. "Dirtyplate1, ready for landing. Over," he said in a muffled voice. "Roger Dirtyplate1, you are clear for landing," he answered in a deeper and even more muffled voice. Dirtyplate1 flew into the open bay of the dock, the name of which had triggered this completely silly daydream.

Calvin flopped back down on the couch and decided to listen to a screech feed that he had overheard some kids at the mall talking about. He wondered what screech music was.

SCREECH-SCREECH-GROWL! SCREECH-SCREECH-GROWL!

He tried to give it a chance, he really did. He hated to think that he was losing touch with the younger crowd. He really wanted to enjoy it, to feel cool and on the forefront of experiencing new and exciting music.

He hated it—really, really hated it. He thought, kids today are raving idiots, I swear. He switched off the feed.

Calvin was lying on his back, staring at the ceiling and wondering how much more time he had until his cat would arrive. Shortly after that, the cat jumped into his lap—both answering his question and freaking him out.

Calvin jumped, scaring the cat and causing it to jump, which scared Calvin again and caused him to jump again, which scared the cat again, and so on. These two were obviously made for each other.

CHAPTER 7

Special

"**I** don't understand what you're talking about," proclaimed Bianca for what Bobford3 felt was the twenty-second time that day—the real number was slightly higher.

Bobford3 was attempting to teach Bianca the same lessons that he had taught to Calvin, but Bianca proved to be an emotional and somewhat distracted pupil. Every time he mentioned anything about artificial intelligences, PCs, display lenses, or anything related to technology (which was everything), he would get this same response from Bianca, and it was getting on his nerves. He then tried explaining the ideas to her as if she were a six-year-old.

"Listen," explained Bobford3, "Ariel is like Santa in that Ariel keeps a list of who's been naughty and who's been nice. The nice people get all the luxuries of life, while the naughty people get the luxury of a quick death. The really naughty people have to listen to screech music until they kill themselves."

A spark of understanding flashed in Bianca's eyes. She replied, "Oh, OK, you should have just said that in the first place. But why are you talking to me about Santa? I'm not six, you know."

Bobford3 bowed and said, "Sorry, I mean no offense."

"None taken."

"Excellent," replied Bobford3. "So anyway, Ariel keeps track of naughty and nice people by the use of karma, which is a formula that evaluates the value of goods, services, and their usefulness to society."

Bobford3 continued his simplified lesson plan by explaining to Bianca about Ariel's distributed architecture (there are little bits of Ariel in everything), PCs (little cell phones stuck behind the ear), and display lenses (sunglasses that show you little pictures). He wondered why people often use the word "little" while explaining something to a child. He surmised that it must be to make the concepts seem small and harmless.

Plowing on with his lesson plan, Bobford3 did his best to explain the concepts of his society to Bianca. While Bianca had an instinctual understanding of karma, she could not connect this concept to that of money. She felt a deep need to know how much money she had to spend, and seemed preoccupied with wanting to go shopping after Bobford3 explained to her that she had no preset spending limit on her karma. She was then positively transfixed on shopping after learning that there was a mall inside of the laboratory complex and, as a result, she could no longer comprehend anything else. Dumb, dumb, dumb, thought Bobford3.

Bobford3 aborted his lessons and decided to take Bianca shopping. He reasoned that a simple person like Bianca would probably cling to Ariel because Ariel would make her decisions for her. She would most likely do whatever Ariel said without question because she would not know what else to do. If that were going to be the case, Bobford3 could safely leave Bianca in the hands of Ariel, and Ariel could guide her through the rest of her life.

"OK, Bianca, I'll tell you what. We just have to do one more thing and then we can go down to the mall."

"What's that?" asked Bianca enthusiastically.

Bobford3 answered, "We have to activate your built-in PC unit."

"Huh?"

Bobford3 wondered if it would be wise to explain to her that while she was frozen, Blick had sectioned off a part of her brain and converted it into an organic Personal Communicator (PC) and it was soon going to be used as processing power for the artificial intelligence that rules their society. He judged, on the whole, no. So how should he explain this to her? He decided to explain it to her the same way he would explain it to a child—he would lie.

"We have discovered that you are a very special girl," explained Bobford3. "We discovered that you have the ability to communicate with Ariel without any external help. It is almost as if your brain were specially developed to be an integral part of the Ariel system."

Bianca smiled with wonder and then frowned with confusion. "Look, Bob, you seem like a nice enough guy, but I really have no idea what you are talking about most of the time." explained Bianca. She cocked her head and squinted a bit and added, "But anyway, OK, I'll bite; I'm special and all. How does this special power of mine work?"

"Well, the first thing we have to do is activate the power. We do that by speaking a passphrase, that is, a phrase that is not likely to come up in the course of normal conversation, and thus, can safely be made the key to unlocking something special."

Bianca looked a little bewildered. Bobford3 clarified, "I'm going to say a spell that will bring out your special power."

Bianca looked unconvinced.

"Now, this may sound a little odd," explained Bobford3, "but just listen to my next sentence and do not interrupt me."

Bianca nodded.

Bobford3 cleared his throat and then spoke the following words clearly, loudly, and distinctly, "I hate eating elephants because they always trample on my tongue."

"What?" demanded Bianca.

"I told you," said Bobford3 factually, "It was going to be a little odd."

Bianca's right temple began to hurt, partly because she was trying to grasp what was going on, but mainly because a capsule had just burst in her brain in response to the passphrase. The capsule contained a few hardworking microbots that were programmed to complete the last stage of rewiring her brain—connecting the user interface. Bianca held her hand up to her forehead in pain and her vision blurred.

Bobford3 put his hand on her shoulder to steady her and said, "You'll be fine in a minute, Bianca. You're just experiencing some momentary side effects from the er . . . spell."

Bianca said nothing. She closed her eyes and leaned back onto the bed. She felt as if she were about to have a migraine. Her head was throbbing and her brain felt swimmy.

Fortunately for her, the pain disappeared as quickly as it had come. She opened her eyes to see Bobford3 leaning over her with his hand still on her shoulder. She sat up slowly so as not to jostle her head and bring back the headache.

"I can see your pores," remarked Bianca.

"I beg your pardon."

"I'm sorry," explained Bianca, "I'm not sure why I said that. It's just that I don't remember seeing the pores of your face before, and it shocked me."

"What?"

"Um," said Bianca, "never mind." She looked down at the palm of her hand and began studying it in worrying detail.

Bobford3 frowned. He watched Bianca as she watched her hand, both of them concentrating very hard.

"Oh, I got it!" shouted Bobford3, causing Bianca's concentration to break and her body to jump. "Sorry. But I know what you're talking about now; your eyesight has been improved."

Bianca brightened. "Yes," she said, "that's it. That must be what it is. Everything seems sharper and more detailed. My eyesight must be better. But how?"

"The spell must have worked," answered Bobford3, grinning.

Bianca smiled. "Oh. Well, that's cool. What else is better on me?"

"Well", said Bobford3 as he took a seat beside Bianca on the bed. "Do you remember me telling you that the Ariel system was something like the Internet?"

"Yes."

"Good. And you remember that Ariel is sort of like a search engine, except that she constantly monitors all the information available to her, filters it, and gives you what you need to know, when you need to know it?"

"Yes," replied Bianca," you said she was a proactive search engine or something."

"Exactly!" enthused Bobford3, "I'm so glad you were listening to me. I was afraid I wasn't getting through."

Bianca replied, "I have been listening, but this is a lot to take in, you know."

"Fair enough," replied Bobford3. "You will have to bear with me. I just want you to understand what is going on so you will be able to function in society. It is imperative that you understand how Ariel works so that she can help you while you get acclimated to this society . . . and guide you through the rest of your life for that matter."

"Ariel sounds very comforting," enthused Bianca.

Bobford3 thought about this. "Yes . . . I rather think she is." He had never really thought about it in those terms before but he had to admit that she had a point.

Bobford3 smiled to himself and continued. "So anyway, to continue with my lesson. You need to be able to communicate with Ariel. Now, most of us use PCs to do this, as I have already explained. But you, you my dear Bianca are special. You now have the ability to communicate with Ariel completely on your own, without any external help. Are you ready to learn how?"

Bianca's eyes twinkled as her head bowed slightly. She answered hesitantly, sheepishly, "Yes, but . . . this isn't going to hurt again, is it?" Her hair draped itself in front of her face, partially obscuring her deep brown eyes.

"No, don't worry about a thing. This will be fun," answered Bobford3. "We will start with something simple, with Ariel communicating to you in text mode. Are you ready?"

Bianca nodded and answered, "Yes."

"OK. Go ahead Ariel."

To Bianca's surprise, the words **Ariel: Hello Bianca. Welcome.** displayed on the bottom of her vision in large, friendly green letters. Wherever she looked, the letters remained just at the bottom of her sight and always in focus.

Bianca squirmed. She looked around her immediate area for something. Bobford3 thought she looked upset.

"Bianca, are you OK?" asked Bobford3.

Bianca looked startled and confused. She asked, "Where is the keyboard? I want to write back."

Bobford3 answered, "Relax, babe. It's OK. Just take . . ."

"Don't call me babe," snapped Bianca.

"Sorry about that sweetie," said Bobford3 with a grin and a pat on her shoulder.

"Don't call me . . . ah, never mind. I can see I'm not going to win this."

"You're right," said Bobford3, "so just try to relax and learn. You are not going to make any friends around here if you're so uptight, sweetie."

"OK, I'll try to relax," muttered Bianca with pouty lips.

Bobford3 raised a questioning eyebrow and said, "OK, great, then to continue. You can talk to Ariel in a couple of ways. The first is by far the simplest method to teach you. You can simply talk to her. Just speak aloud and she will hear you."

"OK," said Bianca, "I'll try it. Here it goes." She cleared her throat and said loudly, "Hello Ariel, how are you?"

The words **Ariel: I am 100% operational, thank you for asking.** displayed on the bottom of her vision in small green letters. Bianca smiled. "That's pretty neat. Can Ariel speak back? Does she have a voice?"

"Of course she does," answered Bobford3. "Ariel, won't you demonstrate for Bianca."

An angelic voice was then heard by Bianca. It said, "I am looking forward to working with you, Bianca. You are a very special person. You are unique."

Because the voice only existed in Bianca's mind, only she could here it in its truest form. Everyone else in the world had to hear Ariel through their PCs, which generated the voice by mechanically vibrating the bones of the ear.

Bianca was indeed unique. She could hear Ariel because her mind was receiving direct communication from a section of itself that was a working part of the Ariel system. One could say, therefore, that she was talking to herself and the voice that she heard was created in her own mind. Her mind, which desperately needed comfort and companionship, created a voice that was the absolute softest, kindest, and most reassuring voice that Bianca could ever imagine.

Bianca smiled in wonder and bliss. She felt safe. She felt warm. She was happy for the first time in a long time, and this feeling of warmth and happiness was quickly ruined by Bobford3's crude remark, which was, "Hey sweet cheeks, you with me?"

Bianca's tranquility was ruined and she wasn't at all happy about it. "Fuck off. Don't call me that! God, I was so happy just now, and you had to go and piss me off. What the hell is your problem? Didn't your mother ever teach you about respect? I bet you can't keep a girlfriend with a mouth like yours. I bet you . . ."

"Whoa, whoa. Sorry! Sorry! Just calm down, alright," protested Bobford3. "I didn't mean anything by it. It is just my way of being endearing. Everyone else thinks it's charming. What's your problem?"

Bianca was more than happy to tell him what her problem was. "I bet you're the boss around here, right?"

"Yes."

"Of course," said Bianca, as if this cleared everything up. "No one is going to tell you to your face that you are a pompous jerk because you're their boss. But you're not my boss, so kindly watch your mouth around me. I think you could treat me with a little more respect, don't you?"

"Listen hot stuff," sneered Bobford3, "You don't know anything about this society and you don't know anything about me. And you sure as hell don't know anything about respect. If it weren't for me, you would be dead right now! You hear me? Dead! Where is my gratitude for that? Where is my respect? I'm trying to teach you about this society. I'm trying to teach you that we are a more informal, nonchalant, and generally relaxed society than you are used to. Now if you don't want to learn to relax, I promise you that you will be dead by sundown.

So I suggest that you get off of your high horse and give me a fucking break!"

Bobford3 had never again seen a woman cry so hard or so long than that day. It took him over an hour to calm her down and make her smile again. He even went as far as to take off his socks and perform a puppet show for her. This seemed to cheer her up, but it was not really because of the impromptu puppet show but because Bobford3 had mismatched socks and she was able to make fun of him for it.

Eventually Ariel decided to intervene. No one is sure exactly what Ariel said to Bianca that day, but we can speculate that it was something like, "Are you really going to let a person with mismatched socks get you upset? Bobford3 can be trying at times, but just look at him; he obviously means well. Look how silly he is willing to be just to make you happy. He is a good guy. Don't be so hard on him," but probably more mechanical.

Bianca glanced over at the other side of the bed. Bobford3 was hidden behind the bed, with only his socked hands exposed. The puppets were engaged in some kind of heavy groping puppet sex, which caught Bianca completely off guard and made her giggle and blush.

"OK, dickhead," said Bianca playfully, "let's get on with the lesson."

Bobford3's head popped up from behind the bed. "Hey, what's with the name calling? Can't we just be friends?"

"Listen," shrugged Bianca, "you have your terms of endearment, and I have mine."

Bobford3 stood again beside the bed and said, "Good to hear it sweet cheeks, good to hear it. Now, do you want to continue learning about your abilities?"

"Of course."

"Excellent. OK. Well, going back to the idea of talking to Ariel. It is all fine and dandy to speak to Ariel aloud, but what if you are in public? No one wants to hear your conversations, and I am fairly sure that you would prefer to keep them private as well.

"Most of us communicate with Ariel by using a touchpad on the inside of our mouth, behind our teeth. Since you have no PC in which to connect such a device, you must communicate with Ariel differently. You have to use your imagination."

"My imagination?" questioned Bianca. "What do you want me to do, invent a way to talk to her? I'm not a scientist, you know."

"No one said that you were, my dear," responded Bobford3 with his trademarked condescension. "However, you can still invent a way to talk to Ariel. You can communicate with Ariel by using your imagination—your mind's eye if you will. It is up to you to invent a way that is most natural for you. Do you want me to give you some examples?"

Bianca was intrigued and confused. "Please," she responded.

"OK, let me see," began Bobford3, "Well, one way you could do it is by imagining the words in your mind. Either one at a time or a whole sentence at a time. It would probably make the most sense for you to picture them down at the bottom of your vision, where Ariel writes to you. Maybe picture them in another color, like red or blue or whatever. Does that sound reasonable?"

Bianca tilted her head and said, "Reasonable, I guess, but very, very weird."

"Try it," encouraged Bobford3.

"OK," said Bianca. She closed her eyes for a moment and then opened them again. "Bob?"

"Yes, what's the matter?"

"I don't know how to spell Ariel."

Bobford3 cracked a smile and spelled it for her. He also told her that the spelling was not very important because as long as she knew what she meant, then Ariel would know as well.

Bianca nodded and closed her eyes again in concentration. Much to Bianca's surprise and gratification, the following words appeared at the bottom of her vision:

Bianca: Hello Ariel, do you read me?
Ariel: Yes, I read you loud and clear.

"That's so amazing," enthused Bianca. "How does it work?"

Bobford3 still didn't think it a good idea to tell Bianca that he and another colleague had mucked about with her brain, and that some of it was now being used to run their entire civilization. Bobford3 smartly dodged the question and suggested that they do some shopping. As he had hoped, the promise of limitless shopping was most effective in changing the subject and so the two of them were quickly bound for the mall.

CHAPTER 8

Glow

For the past five hours, man-made molecules known as alcohol scrubbers had been floating aimlessly inside Tarpa's bloodstream. Occasionally, one of them would bump into an alcohol molecule, where it would make a larger, biochemically inert molecule that would eventually get filtered out of the blood by the liver and find itself in Tarpa's urine. This new molecule would then react to its new acidic environment by fluorescing a vibrant green color.

Although having your urine glow in the dark is now considered a side effect of alcohol scrubbers, these molecules were originally invented for exactly that reason by a few bright college students that thought it would be funny to piss glowing urine from the roof of their fraternity house in celebration of July 4th.

Unfortunately for the students, the compound had the side effect of removing all of the alcohol from their bloodstreams, causing all of them to be too sober to be brave enough to execute their plan. Fortunately, however, their sobriety enabled them to realize that they could market this side effect as the intended purpose of the molecule. This idea earned them all an impressive number of karma points as well as instant popularity with their alcoholic frat brothers because it meant that they could party without hangovers.

Tarpa was unaware that she had been given alcohol scrubbers by the house robot and was more than a little surprised when the toilet began to glow as she used it. To alleviate Tarpa's anxiety, Ariel was then kind enough to explain the phenomenon to her. Tarpa wiped her brow in relief, washed her hands, and left the bathroom.

As Tarpa left the bathroom, Ariel also told her that she had an assignment for her if she was up to the challenge. Tarpa was absolutely up to the challenge and memorized the details of the assignment with glee. This was a perfect opportunity to exercise her new philosophy of life, which was that she existed solely to kill and to do it in the most brutally ironic way imaginable.

Tarpa's next target was a Mrs. Kathy Preston, or Kitty as she liked to be called. Kitty was a middle-aged woman who never quite recovered from her long overdue divorce from her abusive husband. Whether she was more traumatized by the abuse or the divorce is a matter of speculation, but not a matter that is particularly interesting so we will move on to the repercussions of these events.

The day after her divorce, Kitty purchased two small cats from the local pet store with the hope that they would fill the void she felt in her heart. She had planned on buying only one cat, but the one she liked the most had a playmate in the same cage. Not wishing to break up the set, she purchased them both.

Approximately two years later the female cat had a litter of five kittens. This brought the total number of cats to seven. Not wanting to break up a happy family, Kitty kept them all.

Some time after that, a stray cat wondered into Kitty's yard. Kitty thought it was adorable, so she let it join the others. This brought the total number of cats to eight.

This new cat promptly taught the inside cats that it was much easier to go to the bathroom wherever they pleased instead of limiting themselves to the litter box. The inside cats thought this was a wonderful idea and started pissing on anything within their reach. Kitty did her best to re-discipline the cats but it was hard work. Cats are intelligent animals, but they are also lazy. Once one of them decided not to go in the box, the rest of them realized they did not have to go there either. Occasionally, when Kitty would give them fresh litter, they would use the box again—but only because it bothered them that there was somewhere in the house not covered with their scent.

The new cat was also nice enough to impregnate two of the females, later resulting in two more litters. This brought the total number of cats up to seventeen. It was more or less around this time when Mrs. Kathy Preston became known by her neighbors, her family, and some of her friends as "Mrs. Kitty P." It was also the time when her three youngest kids decided it was time to move out.

The increasing health hazard of her house and the decreasing respect among her friends and family caused Kitty to fall into a downward spiral of depression that only served to aggravate the situation. Kitty stopped working and stayed at home watching reruns of daytime talk shows (only reruns existed because the hosts of these shows had long since been terminated) and stuffing her face with junk food. Kitty also stopped cleaning the house entirely.

While several attempts were made to rehabilitate her, Kitty continued to become more of a waste of oxygen than a valuable human being. Her poor attitude and irritable disposition started to severely affect her five children. These five very bright and potentially successful people were being adversely affected by one dim and definitely unsuccessful person, so it was a simple calculation on Ariel's part to order the hit.

Tarpa was intent on making this assignment something special—not only to make her life more exciting, but also to bury her conflicted thoughts about Calvin's reappearance.

She fretted. She frowned. She bit her nail. She hurt her tooth biting her nail. She paced. She fretted some more.

She smiled. She had devised her plan. She found her backpack and filled it with the following items: gas mask, nail file, funnel, kitty litter, glitter, sardines, bar of soap, milk, two Sony PatientMen, baked beans, rope, change of clothes, duct tape, glue, tubing, shampoo, some kind of gizmo, and lemon juice.

With her plan roughed out, Tarpa went for a walk along the beach to sort out the details in her mind, to tone the muscles in her legs, and to put some ocean air into her lungs.

CHAPTER 9

Shopping

"Wow, it's very pretty out today," Bianca observed. Bobford3 was not at all used to dealing with simple people, so he did not see the obvious reason why Bianca had made such a comment.

"How do you know it's a nice day out?" asked Bobford3 innocently.

Bianca glanced upward, as if checking her facts, then answered triumphantly, "Because the sun is out, stupid." She pointed at the ceiling of the mall.

Bobford3 covered his face with his hand while he composed himself. "You know that you are in a mall right now, don't you?" asked Bobford3 challengingly.

Bianca looked around and saw caves burrowed into the surrounding mountainsides, and inside those caves, she saw clothing racks. She answered, "Yes, I figured we are at the mall. I mean, I see those funky stores built into the cliff side. Pretty neat. A little primitive, but neat. I thought this was supposed to be the future. Oh well, but anyway, I know we are at the mall. I also know we are outside."

Bobford3 gave a sarcastic huff and said, "Did you happen to notice on which floor we left the elevator?"

Bianca shook her head.

"We are on the eleventh floor of my building. We are still inside the building. Inside."

Bianca looked around again in puzzlement and said, "It must be a very large building."

Bobford3 put his hand on her shoulder and said, "All an optical allusion, sweet cheeks." Bianca briskly swatted his hand off her shoulder and huffed." Bobford3 bowed to her slightly and said, "I'm sorry, Bianca. I just have to learn to see things on your le . . ." he stopped and corrected himself, ". . . I mean, from your point of view." He didn't want to insult her by implying that he was operating on a higher level than she, even though he knew it was true.

Bianca smiled. "It's OK," she said, "I should learn not to take what I am seeing for granted. I'm sure there are plenty of things that I will not instantly comprehend, so please bear with me."

"I will," answered Bobford3. "So, how about some shopping?"

Bianca smiled.

"I'll wait here," said Bobford3, "and you go look around." Bobford3 was not the type of man who enjoyed following women while they aimlessly meandered from store to store, never finding exactly what they were looking for because such a thing simply did not exist. In other words, he was a sane man.

Bianca meandered aimlessly from store to store, not finding what she was looking for because she had no idea what she was looking for—but she would know it when she saw it.

In fact, she saw it now. It was a long, silky, flowing dress. The dress had a surprisingly realistic island beach scene printed on it, which gave it a very Polynesian look. The scene was so detailed that it could pass as three dimensional. Adding to the effect of realism was an ocean that lapped up and down on a white sandy beach while palm trees swayed gently in the breeze. Bianca had to have it.

She gently lifted the dress by the hanger, admiring its beauty and its technology. The image faded into a new image, an image of a lush green tropical jungle beside a mountainside with a huge rushing waterfall splashing down the side of it. Bianca really had to have the dress.

She took the dress up to the counter, or rather, she tried to take the dress up to the counter, but she couldn't find one anywhere in the store. She asked one of the other customers of the store if they knew where the counter was, but she simply shrugged and said she never heard of that store. When Bianca tried to explain to her that she wanted to pay for the dress, the customer merely shrugged again and casually slinked off in another direction, hoping not to be followed by the crazy lady.

Bianca heard a soft, angelic voice in her head. The voice said, "Bianca, you do not have to worry about paying for the dress. It is yours if you want it."

Bianca said, "Oh thank you," which caused people near her to stare at her for a second and then slink off in other directions, hoping not to be followed by the crazy lady.

Bianca then realized that the voice was that of Ariel's. She covered up her mouth and giggled, her cheeks getting red with embarrassment. She felt the urge to answer vocally, but suppressed it. Remembering her lesson from Bobford3, she closed her eyes and imagined the words she wanted to say.

Bianca: I can't possibly accept a gift. I hardly even know you.
Ariel: It is not a gift. You will pay for it with karma. Actually, if you prefer, you can think of it as coming from Bobford3. I am deducting some of his karma because of his lack-luster job in teaching you the basics.

Bianca didn't know what to make if this, but she wasn't about to turn down a gift.

Bianca: Oh. Thank you. That is very kind.
Ariel: It is not kind; it is fair. Is there anything else I can help you with?

Bianca shook her head no. Then she said, "Wait, I do have a question." She saw the stares of scared strangers again. "Damn. Oops. Damn it."

She took a calming breath and spoke to Ariel in text mode, which she did not really have to do because the store was now empty.

Bianca: Ariel, what kind of dress is this?

Bianca held up the silky dress. It was now showing a night sky with twinkling stars.

Ariel: It is a fabrision dress.
Bianca: I've never heard of him. He must be new.
Ariel: Fabrision is not a designer. It is a style of dress. The fabric is made from woven cardion. Cardion is a strong, carbon-based material similar to diamond. It can be manufactured in long, threadlike fibers that are capable of channeling light. The thread is as smooth as silk but even stronger. All of the fibers in the dress begin at the bottom hem of the dress, but they end in a compact grid covering the entire dress. A thin layer of material covers this network of fiber as protection. Images are created in the bottom hem of the dress, carried by the network of fibers, and displayed on the surface of the dress. The images can be anything the wearer wishes, and the system is self-powered by the motion of the dress as it is worn.
Bianca: I'll take two.

Bianca left that store and entered another. This one was extravagantly decorated with plush, burgundy walls and lacy, gold trim. The floor was sterling silver with a golden logo embossed in the center of it.

The logo was circular. The outside diameter of it was comprised of what appeared to Bianca to be the plastic that held six-packs together, but they were joined together end-to-end like links in a chain. Inside was a jumble of images that bled together to form one large Rorschach test.

Bianca squinted while trying to make out some of the shapes. A few of the things she spotted were: a milk jug, a fork, a chair, and the dashboard from a Ford Transit van (although, she was a little uncertain about the last one).

She moved her attention over to the contents of this extravagant room, which to her surprise and confusion was primarily filled with plastic patio furniture. As she looked, she realized that this rich-looking store was indeed filled with more crappy plastic items than a dollar store. Everything, absolutely everything, was plastic—chairs, tables, knives, spoons, forks, plates, cups, floor tiles, statues, lamps—everything.

She read the border of the sign in hopes of discovering the nature of the store by its name. The name was "Nicolette's Antiques." Antiques? Plastic antiques? She shook her head and left. Antique or not, she was not interested in dollar store junk—not with an unlimited karma limit to work with.

She never thought that she would feel this way before, but Bianca suddenly really didn't feel like shopping anymore. She was feeling a little nauseous from this morning and the strain of trying to decipher her new surroundings was giving her a nasty headache.

Bianca backtracked to where she had left Bobford3. He was chatting with a pretty young girl that was sitting beside him on the bench. Bianca crept behind the bench, leaned over Bobford3's shoulder and kissed him on the cheek, and then said, "I'm sorry I took so long my love." The young girl stopped in mid-sentence, gave Bobford3 a disdainful look, and walked away in a huff.

Bobford3 rounded on her and said, "You are just pure evil."

Bianca smirked. "Sorry, I get a little mischievous when I'm nervous."

"It's not your best quality, I'll tell you that," said Bobford3. "How about I take you back to your room? You can take a nice hot bath and relax a little—for both of our sakes."

Bianca thought that sounded like a top-ten idea, so she went cheerily back to Room 8 of the laboratory with Bobford3. She tried her best to relax in the hot tub, which she would normally have found quite soothing, but unfortunately the hot tub kept telling her all of its troubles and why all of its misery was the direct result of the actions of humanity. Needless to say, she was even grumpier after her shortened bath.

She still felt sick, and her head was spinning from the odd stores that she had seen and the odd bath that she had just taken. She lay down on the bed, hid under the covers and tried fitfully to fall asleep.

CHAPTER 10

Timber!

It was Calvin's first day back on the job, and it was raining the kind of misty rain that seemed to catch Calvin in the face no matter which direction he turned. Calvin would have normally been extremely irritated by this, but the beauty of his surroundings engulfed his attention.

The mist enhanced an effect created by the refraction of light through the transparent frames of the various buildings interspersed around the city's park-like landscape. Calvin gaped as colored light-rays danced around the city. The light show was so immensely beautiful that it was even rumored that Jesus Christ would sometimes come down to Earth just to watch it; some even said that if you squinted just right, you could see him in the tree tops. No one seriously believed it, though.

After watching the lights for a while, Calvin decided that he better start earning some karma. He walked to the dark-red trail, which was his patch of patrol area. He patrolled up and down the trail for over an hour ensuring that everyone and everything was OK. Not many people were walking the trails in the rain, but rather more sensibly traveling underground in the ODIN tunnels. As a result, Calvin was extremely bored. His mind wandered and he started thinking about his crazy new life.

Calvin wondered what his new life was going to be like. Was he ever going to make any friends that he could relate to? Was Ariel ever going to let him date anyone, and would anyone want to be with him if she did? He wondered if he would ever fit in.

He wondered if he would ever be happy here. He wondered if he should be concerned that a large tree was crashing toward him out of the forest.

—CRASH—

As his life flashed before his eyes, he saw clearly that the answers to his questions were: Probably yes, probably yes, probably no, probably no, probably no, and definitely yes.

A tree falling on someone is a surprisingly amusing thing to watch, assuming, of course, that you are not the one under the tree. Someone other than Calvin did, in fact, see the tree fall on him and he was in hysterics, which was a shame because Calvin could have really used some help.

Calvin tried to free himself from the tree, but gravity was giving him a hard time with it. He was just too weak and did not have enough leverage to do anything about the oppressive piece of lumber draped across his chest—not to mention that he was unable to breathe and was feeling a little light-headed as a result.

Ariel felt the need to intervene at this point by asking the hysterically laughing gentleman to please try to get the tree off Calvin. The gentleman obliged. He wiped the tears of laughter from his eyes with one hand and lifted the fallen tree with the other.

Calvin would have normally been extremely impressed with this show of strength and nonchalance, but he was too busy not breathing at that moment. The gentleman finished wiping the tears from his eyes and then pulled Calvin free of the tree. He tossed the tree safely aside with no more effort than if he were tossing a pencil.

After some work, the gentleman was able to resuscitate Calvin and get him semi-conscious. Calvin silently looked around with some confusion in his eyes. He eventually saw the tree and remembered what had happened to him. He then looked back at the gentleman for an explanation.

Noticing the gesture, the gentleman began to explain, "Hey buddy, my name's Tom. You probably figured out by now that you were hit by a tree. You have to watch out for that around here, those buggers can be lethal. Can't say I ever actually saw it happen before, though. Really caught me off guard, it did. Funniest damn thing I ever seen in my life—the dumb look on your face, the flailing arms, all priceless in my book."

Calvin briefly wondered why God hated him so much and then he willed himself unconscious again. Ariel asked Tom if he could please bring Calvin to Bobcorp3. Tom was reluctant to say yes because he was going to meet with some of his friends in a few minutes to get stoned and watch the light show. In the end, his conscience got the best of him and he hefted Calvin's lifeless body all the way back to the moon.

After Tom and Calvin had left the area, a man with a scraggly beard emerged from the upper branches of the fallen tree, wiping dirt from his white robe and pulling twigs out of his long, tangled, brown hair. He looked around like he was embarrassed to be there, and then seemingly disappeared into the mist.

CHAPTER 11

Kitty

lick, Flick, Flick. "Never a fucking thing on the TV to watch. I'm tired of fucking reruns. Why don't they ever make more of them shows about runaway pregnant lesbian teenagers and such like anymore?" asked a haggard, middle-aged woman as she cycled through the thousands of new shows available for her to watch. The cat that she had been talking to simply tilted its head to the side and then rubbed it briskly across the fabric of the couch. Seeing this gesture, Kitty said, "That's right Big Paws, they're all a bunch of fucks," and crammed something orange and crunchy into her mouth. She had orange stains on the corner of her mouth from all the other orange, crunchy things that had been crammed there before. Kitty let Big Paws lick the stains from her mouth and then continued to flick through the stations. Shortly thereafter, she received her twenty-third Bad Karma alert from Ariel, which she ignored like all the others.

Outside of Kitty's house, Tarpa was humming a happy little song while connecting a piece of rubber tubing to a tank of sleeping gas. She connected the other end of the tubing into the fresh air inlet of Kitty's climate control system and turned on the gas.

Tarpa ate a leisurely breakfast on the front lawn of Kitty's house while seventeen smelly cats and one haggard woman fell blissfully asleep inside. Occasionally, a curious neighbor would wander past the house and try to pump Tarpa for information.

Whenever this happened, Tarpa would simply fix them with an icy stare and continue to eat her breakfast and hum her happy little tune.

The appearance of a strange woman on Kitty's lawn had sparked the neighborhood's imagination. While the neighbors were perfectly aware of the existence of the Karma Police, the idea that they were living, breathing people seemed strange to them. As far as they had known, no one they knew had ever been a victim of the police, and certainly never anyone in their neighborhood. However, all of Kitty's neighbors had always joked around with each other that if anyone was ever a candidate for their services, Kitty would be on the top of their list. They all went back into their houses, turned off their lights, peeked out of their curtains, and let their imaginations work overtime, each hoping that the Karma Police were going to do their job.

It was normally Tarpa's style to confront her targets at nighttime to keep her identity a secret from the public. These confrontations were usually extremely violent in nature and never ended happily. She felt it best to keep all of that unpleasantness a secret. However, Tarpa was getting tired of hiding who she was.

In all the years that Tarpa had kept her second job a secret, it never got her anywhere. Tarpa could never make friends, and frankly, she was tired of trying. Everyone she met was almost instantly intimidated by her aggressive disposition and never felt comfortable enough around her to be her friend. Most of the people she knew were only nice to her because she was the sort of person that was useful to have on one's side, but none of them were true friends to Tarpa.

Tarpa was now in a sort of Zen, nothing-really-matters style trance. She had reached a point in her life where she utterly and completely failed to give a shit. So now, she would flaunt the darker side of her lifestyle. Now, she would play with her victims as if they were petty little toys for her amusement. She was determined to be more relaxed and to enjoy every day as much as she possibly could. Today she was going to have a good day.

With her mind thinking happy thoughts and her mouth humming happy tunes, Tarpa cheerily duct taped Kitty's mouth shut and dragged her limp body down into the basement by the hair. Tarpa was wearing a gas mask, which not only served to prevent her from breathing the sleeping gas but also the nasty stench that permeated the house.

Tarpa tied Kitty's hands and feet together. She went back upstairs to locate the litter box. After finding the litter box in the laundry room, she grabbed it and brought it into the backyard where she dumped it upside down on the grass and gave it a good kick to knock out the majority of the crap. She then propped it against the side of the house and rinsed it with the garden hose.

The neighbors watched all of this from the safety of their houses. They were now speculating that Tarpa was not going to kill Kitty after all, but was merely there to clean the house. This was not quite as satisfying to the neighbors because it meant that they would still have to tolerate Kitty on the occasions when she left the house, but at least they wouldn't have to smell that wretched stench coming from her house anymore.

Tarpa waved to the neighbors and then walked back inside the house with the litter box in hand. The neighbors all ducked behind their curtains and wondered how Tarpa had spotted them.

Tarpa went back into the laundry room. She pulled the glue out of her backpack and used it to glue the litter box to the laundry room floor. After the glue was dry (approximately five seconds), she used her arm-knife to slice a hole in the bottom of the litter box and the floor. The cut piece fell into the basement and landed next to Kitty's motionless body. Tarpa peered down into the hole and said, "Don't worry, dear; I'll be right down to take care of you."

Tarpa trial fit the funnel into the hole in the litter box. After some trimming, she was able to press-fit the funnel into the hole where it rested by its rim. Tarpa ran a bead of glue around the rim of the funnel to insure that the funnel stayed in place. She then removed the kitty litter from her backpack and scattered a dusting of it inside the litter box, being careful not to dump any into the funnel.

Now back in the basement, Tarpa tied two ropes to the two beams that ran on either side of the hole that she had just created. She untied Kitty's hands and feet, only to tie each of her hands to each of the ropes attached to the beams of the ceiling. Tarpa carefully adjusted the ropes so that Kitty's head was directly below the hole in the ceiling.

Tarpa attached a length of tubing to the end of the funnel. She cut a hole in the duct tape that was covering Kitty's mouth and inserted the other end of the tube into Kitty's mouth. She added some more pieces of duct tape to each end of the tube to ensure that it stayed in place.

Tarpa now had just a few final changes left. The first of which was to cover Kitty's legs with a thin layer of glue, then sprinkle them with silver glitter. She also needed to place the cats, so she went back upstairs to fetch the six youngest ones. She needed playful kittens to do the basement work.

Tarpa gently placed the kittens around the basement and then carefully filed their front claws to sharp points. She also left them a plate of sardines and a bowl of fresh water.

With the kittens taken care of, she simply had to plug a PatientMan into the gizmo, fill the gizmo full of lemon juice, and aim the resulting contraption at Kitty. Tarpa tried a few test fires of the gizmo, which was originally a device used to hydrate coma patients but was now a makeshift lemon juice sprayer. The gizmo sprayed lemon juice directly onto Kitty's legs at Tarpa's command.

Perfect, the basement was all set. Tarpa went upstairs, closing the basement door behind her. She left a plate of sardines, a plate of baked beans, and a bowl of milk for the upstairs cats to eat in the hopes that they would get smelly diarrhea from the mixture.

It was a simple matter now to place a PatientMan in a spot with a clear view of the litter box, open some of the windows to let the gas out, and leave the house. Tarpa did all of the above with ease.

Once outside of the house, Tarpa removed her gas mask and all of her clothing, threw her clothing in a pile on the front lawn, and lit the pile on fire because God knows she could never get the smell out of them.

Now completely naked, Tarpa gave the neighbors quite a show as she used the garden hose as a makeshift shower. She soaped up with the bar of soap that she had brought from home, which was intended for camping use, and rinsed herself clean with the garden hose. She also shampooed her hair five times before she was convinced that it was clean.

Many of the women inside neighboring houses were swatting their husbands and pulling them away from the curtains. Tarpa gave them all a friendly wave hello then put on a fresh set of clothes.

While she was hosing down the fire, Tarpa observed the feeds from the house to verify that they met with her satisfaction. Tarpa was, in fact, completely satisfied with the feeds and was giddy with the anticipation of watching her plan unfold. She returned to her car and left for home, singing a little ditty she had composed entitled "My Kitty is All Tied Up Tonight".

When Tarpa was halfway home, she received the following message from Ariel:

Ariel: Tarpa, Operation TC1 is a success. Calvin is being transported to Bobcorp3 for experimentation. Please reroute accordingly.

Tarpa was thrilled at how well the day was going for her. She changed her destination to the Moon and amused herself along the way by composing silly little ditties such as "I Fell Harder for Calvin than an Oak in the Woods".

CHAPTER 12

Grumpy

Calvin regained consciousness later that afternoon. He looked at his surroundings and realized that he was right back in Room 7 again! This was becoming a reoccurring nightmare of his.

He was instantly annoyed at what fate or God or the universe was doing to him. He reached for the PatientMan and hurled it at the door with all of his might, but Tarpa caught it before it got there. Calvin started in surprise. Where the hell had she come from? He blinked.

"It's a good thing that you throw like a girl and that I move like a bullet; these things are major karma points," said Tarpa while holding a blue sphere in the palm of her hand. She smirked, but Calvin did not respond. "You're getting to be a grumpy old man these days," she added.

Calvin let a few seconds pass before responding to Tarpa in the hopes of adding emphasis to his words. He then said, "Let me stab you in the heart, kill you dead, bring you back to life, and then drop an oak tree on your chest—then let's see how god damn chipper you feel after that!" His face turned bright red.

Tarpa merely shrugged and answered demurely, "I never dropped a tree on you; it was an act of God."

Calvin knew that she had intentionally missed the point, which only aggravated him further. He looked about the room for something else to throw, but there was nothing nearby, so he settled for heaving the nightstand over and watching it slide into the wall on the opposite side of the room. He also got in a nice, loud, "Damn this place."

"Feel better?"

"Actually," said Calvin, "yes. So what brings you here? Just stopping by to stab me in the heart so we can repeat this fun little game I laughingly call my life?"

"No," answered Tarpa, "but I would be more than happy to accommodate you if you keep acting like a cynical little brat."

"Did I mention that a tree fell on me today? I think you missed that part. A tree, you see, fell right down on my chest and suffocated me nearly to death, all the while I was being laughed at. Laughed at! I think I can afford to be a little cynical, don't you think?" explained Calvin.

"I guess," said Tarpa. "I'm just in a very good mood today and I was hoping that no one was going to spoil it, and now here you are being Mr. Grumpy Pants when all I really want to do is to ask you if you want to have a nice dinner with me tonight."

How does she do that? How does she flip things around so fast? How does she manipulate me so easily? Oh yeah, because she's a hot girl and I'm a big dumb-ass. I keep forgetting.

Calvin refused to apologize for his behavior, but he was willing to meet her halfway by accepting her invitation for dinner.

"Great," said Tarpa, "We'll meet here at seven o'clock. Is that good for you?"

"Yeah, that's cool."

"Excellent. I just have to run a few tests to make sure that you're OK." Tarpa picked up the nightstand and returned it to its place beside Calvin's bed. She then placed the PatientMan on top of it while telling Calvin that if he broke this one, she would stab him in the head. She said it with a smile, but Calvin was not convinced that she was kidding.

Tarpa studied the information from the PatientMan. "Hmm, that's interesting," she said as she peered at Calvin with a puzzled expression. She noticed that Calvin had a fractured rib, and she was very curious why it had not healed.

"What?" asked Calvin in response to the concerned look.

"Tell me Calvin;" asked Tarpa, "did they give you anything when you got here—any medication?"

"What? I don't know, why?"

Tarpa frowned. "Never Mind, I'll ask Ariel"

Tarpa: Ariel, was Calvin given any nano-rebuilders upon his arrival to the lab?

Ariel: Yes, he was given pain killers, nano-rebuilders, and nano-cams at 12:31 PM.

Tarpa looked down in thought. Calvin stared at her intently, trying to figure out what she was thinking.

Tarpa looked back at Calvin and asked, "When was the last time that you drank Tang?"

Calvin frowned and answered sarcastically, "Hmm, let me see. I don't know—it seems like a lifetime ago. Oh yes, that's right, it was a lifetime ago. It was the day you killed me. Wednesday if my memory is correct."

Tarpa ignored his sad little plea for sympathy and recorded the information. It had been four days since Calvin had consumed the Tang.

Calvin watched as Tarpa stared off into space while she worked on the Ariel system. He asked her what Tang had to do with anything, but she gave him no more than a, "Shh". Calvin eyed the PatientMan. One more minute, he told himself, and then I'm gonna smash that thing.

Tarpa asked Ariel to approximate Calvin's Tang intake from the time that he had first been revived to the present. She then plotted that data with an estimate of the damage to Calvin's body that had been inflicted over the same time period. She then smoothed the graph to get an estimate of the healing power of Tang per milliliter.

"I'm sorry," said Tarpa while turning her attention back to Calvin, "What were you saying?"

"What is the deal with the Tang? What are you so concerned about?"

Tarpa gently shook her head. "Not concerned, just curious. Do you remember me telling you about Bobford3's hypothesis about Tang, about how it helped us to revive you?"

"Yes?"

"Well, I think it is correct. In fact, I think that the Tang is helping you to heal faster, but I'm not sure how. I mean, I have my suspicions, but I'd like to try something if it is OK with you."

"What?" asked Calvin. "It isn't going to hurt, is it?"

"No, I just want you to drink some Tang."

"Oh. That's it? Yeah, I can do that for you. I'm actually thirsty anyway."

"OK," said Tarpa, "I'll be right back."

Tarpa left Calvin's room for a moment while she went to the kitchen to retrieve the Tang, only to return a few minutes later with a glass of unnaturally orange liquid that had been precisely measured per her calculations. She gave it to Calvin.

—GULP—

As Calvin guzzled down the Tang, Tarpa watched the feed from tiny little cameras that Calvin had swallowed earlier, thinking they were aspirin.

"Hey Calvin, check out the feed from inside your body."

"My what?" demanded Calvin.

"Ariel, show Calvin the feed."

The feed featured Calvin's fractured rib. It was partially obscured by a cloudy coating that Tarpa recognized to be the nano-rebuilders. But they weren't rebuilding squat.

Tarpa was not sure why they weren't mending the break. The rebuilders carried with them all the usual proteins needed to rebuild living tissue. They could decode the DNA in the surrounding cells and repair them or create replacement cells with a minimum of fuss, so why weren't they doing it?

Suddenly, the cloud began to lighten as the rebuilders began to head for a different part of the body. Tarpa immediately ordered the cameras to follow them. She watched as the rebuilders made their way to Calvin's stomach.

Tarpa watched in amazement as the rebuilders jettisoned their protein stores and began to gather up some molecules of the xanthan and cellulose gums present in the Tang mixture that was swilling around in Calvin's stomach.

The rebuilders then raced their way back to the fracture. The cloud reappeared around Calvin's rib. Tarpa watched as it swarmed feverishly around the fracture.

At first, Tarpa still thought that the rebuilders were ineffective because she couldn't notice any improvement in the fracture. She then assumed that the rebuilding was just too slow to see with the naked eye.

She took note of the damage, closed her eyes to the count of ten, and opened them again. Yes, the fracture did look a bit smaller. She tried it again. Yes, it was working! But why?

After nearly three minutes of work, the rebuilders had seamlessly repaired Calvin's rib. Calvin was dumbfounded and expressed it eloquently by screaming, "Holy shit!"

Tarpa jerked to attention and refocused on Calvin, who was punching himself in the chest.

"Dude, I'm freaking indestructible!"

"Yes, well, it's just a shame your brain is still damaged."

"You're just jealous."

Tarpa responded, "I'm not jealous; I look at it as a challenge."

Calvin squinted and asked, "Just what do you mean by that?"

"Nothing," responded Tarpa with a smirk. She quickly changed the subject. "So, did you really understand what just happened?"

"Yes, Tang just healed my fractured rib in a matter a minutes."

"Not quite," replied Tarpa. "We gave you some nano-rebuilders when you arrived here, and they did the repair on your rib. They were the gray dust that was swarming around the fracture. But, it seems that your cells now have a protective coating of Tang and are very resistant to damage. When your rib was cracked, very few cells were damaged; instead they were merely separated from each other. The rebuilders had realized that fact and used the Tang that you had swallowed as glue to repair the fracture."

Calvin thought about this. "Bull shit," he answered. "How can infinitely small machines possibly have enough intelligence to know to use Tang to glue my mutant cells together?"

Tarpa squinted. "That's a bloody good question. I mean, they know enough to look around the body for excess materials that they can use in reconstruction, but the only way they could have possibly known to use Tang was if it were mapped into your DNA. But if that's true, then . . ." Tarpa paused to collect her thoughts.

"Then what?" demanded Calvin.

"Then that means that you are correct; you really do have mutant cells. They are, in fact, genetically predisposed to be resin coated," answered Tarpa.

"Oh, so that's why it says 'Made in China' on my ass," joked Calvin.

Tarpa smiled and added, ". . . and 'Fisher Price' on your forehead."

Calvin didn't bother to respond.

Tarpa paced around to the other side of the bed. "So, aren't you going to ask me about the camera?"

"Nah."

"You really don't care that we put cameras inside of your body?" asked Tarpa.

"No," answered Calvin. "I figured you guys probably had something like that. They are very nice."

"Nice?" exclaimed Tarpa, slightly affronted. "Nice? They are the single most complicated to fabricate machines that have ever been created! I had hoped for more enthusiasm from you."

Calvin backpedaled, "Hey, I didn't mean to belittle them. I just took it for granted that they existed. But I suppose if I knew how complicated they were to build, I would have had a greater respect for them. Sorry, I didn't know."

"No problem. Hey, I have to go check up on one of my projects. Do you need anything before I go?"

"I guess not," answered Calvin. "No, wait. I wanted to ask you something. This may sound a little silly, but I was wondering if I could have some mods done. Specifically, I'd like the same electro-muscular implants that you have—well, without the capacitors. I'd also like a liquid nitrogen sprayer implanted in the same manor as your arm-knife."

"What are you going to do with that stuff, hunt squirrels?" mocked Tarpa.

"No, little miss sarcasm. I'm going to use the liquid nitrogen to battle forest fires, and the electro-muscular implants to save myself and others from harm, like say a tree falls on someone or something."

Tarpa shrugged. "Sounds reasonable enough to me, but you will have to ask Ariel."

Calvin shrugged back. "OK. So Ariel, can I have that stuff?"

Ariel's creepy ghost voice answered inside of Calvin's head, "Yes, as long as you do not use the equipment to harm anyone unless you have permission from me to do so."

Calvin turned his attention back to Tarpa. "She said yes. When can I go under the knife?"

Tarpa did a few calculations and answered, "I'd say around this time tomorrow—and no Tang for you until after the surgery!"

"Why?"

Tarpa answered, "Because you have rebuilders inside of your body and they last for about a month. So every time we cut into you or modify you, the little bastards are going to keep healing you up while we work. Our only hope is to wait until all the Tang is out of your body so that the rebuilders have nothing to fix you with. I'll have to consult Bobford3 about what materials he thinks we should use so that the rebuilders leave our equipment alone after the surgery, especially after you guzzle down some Tang."

Calvin responded, "Oh, yeah, that makes sense."

Tarpa noticed the time and said with hurry in her voice, "Hey, I really have to get going now. I'll see you tonight, OK?"

"Sure thing, I'll be looking forward to it."

Tarpa bent over and gave him a light kiss on the mouth. "Bye sweetie."

"Bye."

After Tarpa left the room, Calvin allowed himself to float on cloud nine for a moment. Eventually, his cynical side told him to cut it out. It also told him that she would probably just kill him again or something so he shouldn't get his hopes up. Damn his cynical side, he thought.

Calvin, now bored and alone, decided to pass the time until his dinner date with Lady Death by watching some television. He flipped to the same Evionia feed that he had stumbled upon the day before, and instantly regretted it.

The feed showed two men with mullet haircuts siphoning off a clear but cloudy liquid from a large metal vat. The liquid then emptied into a strange entanglement of glassware and surgical tubing. Under some of the glassware was a moderate fire which evaporated the liquid into vapor. The vapor then traveled through some tubing and condensed into another glass jug while wondering why it even bothered to go through all the trouble of evaporating in the first place. The liquid then emptied into a wooden mug and then down the throat of one of the mullet-wearing men who had just lost at Rock-Paper-Scissors.

After a lengthy coughing spell, the man began complaining about his eyesight going funny. It was more or less at this time when Calvin decided to find another feed.

The next feed was even more puzzling to Calvin. It was a split video feed with one image on top and one on the bottom. But that wasn't what was puzzling Calvin. What puzzled Calvin were the images themselves.

The top video, and the more mundane of the two, was a view which looked down at the floor of a room which contained a few box-shaped machines, a litter box, and a dazed and bedraggled cat, which was walking toward the litter box with suspicion. The litter box was centered in the view and Calvin could see that it had a hole in the center of it, which he thought was rather odd. Calvin would have assumed that the hole emptied into some fancy, litter-box-cleaning machine, had he not seen the bottom view.

The bottom view was an altogether scarier scene and seeing it caused Calvin to wonder if he had stumbled onto someone's home bondage video, but like a trooper he kept watching. The main feature of the video was a middle-aged woman, slightly overweight and completely unkempt. She was centered on the bottom video, just below the top video of the litter box. Her hands were tied to the beams of the ceiling. Her mouth was taped shut, but she could still breathe through her nose. There was also a length of tubing that stretched from a hole in the ceiling to a hole in the tape that covered her mouth, which she could presumably breathe though as well.

Calvin was completely disgusted to realize that the hole in the litter box shown in the top video was the entrance to the tube leading to the woman's mouth in the bottom video. The thought of it made Calvin dry-heave, but like a trooper he kept watching.

In the room with the woman were a number of cats, most of which were transfixed on the woman's legs—not because they were particularly beautiful, but because they sparkled as if they had been covered with glitter.

Whenever the woman would wiggle around in an effort to free herself from the ropes, her legs would catch the attention of some of the cats, which would, in turn, scratch the hell out of her legs. When they did this, the woman would panic and flail her legs, which would continue the ugly cycle.

Calvin watched for several minutes as the woman struggled with her situation. Eventually, the woman realized that if she kept as still as possible, the cats would leave her alone. Unfortunately for the woman, it was not going to be that easy because, little did she know, a cat with a belly full of warm milk and sardines was now stepping into the litter box which led directly into her mouth. Calvin saw this and dry-heaved again. But like a trooper, he kept watching.

The cat featured in the top video sniffed around the litter box for a short while and then jumped in. Because of the hole in the center of the litter box, it had to stand on the outskirts of the box with its face pointing outward, thus positioning its rear end directly over the hole. No longer able to hold it, the cat released its belly full of spoiled milk and half-digested sardines directly into the hole.

The fowl smelling, chunky, brown liquid crept its way down the tube and slid sickeningly into the mouth of the woman below. Calvin wanted to close his eyes or turn off the feed, but like a trooper he kept watching.

The woman was, as you would suspect, not at all happy when the liquid made its way into her mouth. She had no idea what it was, only that it was dreadful and that it made her gag. She coughed and sputtered and eventually gagged so much that she threw up, which only added to her disgust because there was now so much fluid in her mouth and in the tube that she was about to drown if she didn't swallow it all.

As the lady twitched and writhed in disgust, she flailed her legs around, provoking the ferocious kittens to attack once again. They tore into her flesh for several minutes, leaving her legs bloody and throbbing. The woman could stand no more of this torture and was on the verge of passing out when Tarpa, who was also watching the feed, chose that moment to activate the lemon juice sprayers. The woman spasmed in pain and willfully passed out—to Tarpa's complete satisfaction and to Calvin's complete horror.

Calvin, no longer a trooper, switched off the feed and curled up in a ball on his bed, hugging his pillow for comfort. Tarpa, on the other hand, hummed a happy tune as she made her way home to get ready for her dinner date.

CHAPTER 13

Date

"Listen Calvin, I'm a working girl," said Tarpa in a moodily lit bistro.

"You're a prostitute?"

"No, no. That's not what I meant. I mean that I'm a girl who places her work above all else—a workaholic. And as such I have no place in my life for a serious relationship."

"This is meant to be polite dinner conversation?" asked Calvin.

"I promised dinner. I never mentioned the tone of the accompanying conversation," replied Tarpa before continuing. "So here is the deal: I like you, Calvin," she stared off while shaking her head and added, "although I don't for the life of me know why."

Calvin screwed up his face at her.

Tarpa continued, "You make me feel soft and warm—and I like that, but it scares the hell out of me. I can't have that in my life every day. I'm a killer, Calvin. I can't be a soft and warm killer. It just wouldn't work. But a girl has needs, you know. And you seem to be the only person I've met who is, well, either brave or stupid enough not to be scared of me. So here's the deal. I am going to come over to your place from time to time for some quality time. We can hang out sometimes too, but I don't want you to get all clingy with me. And to be clear—when I want my space, I get it."

"Um, I'm sorry, are you a guy? I mean, have you been surgically altered into a woman or something? Please don't tell me you used to be a guy—because that was a totally guy thing to say."

Tarpa shrugged and then leaned forward over the table. She spoke in a meek voice, "Well, um, if you want to split hairs . . ."

"Yes . . ."

". . . and go with the percentages . . ."

"Yes . . ." Calvin's forehead was now sweating.

". . . Then . . ."

"Yes?"

"Then I'm a robot."

"Huh?!?"

"I'm 65% machine because of all my mods," explained Tarpa.

"I don't give a crap about that. As long as the outside is soft and squishy and female, it's fine. What I'm asking is, were you born a man?"

Tarpa leaned forward and playfully choked Calvin with one hand while saying, "Of course I have always been a woman. And if you ever ask me that again, I'll surgically alter you with my own bare hands."

Tarpa released his neck and sat back. Calvin had five partial puncture wounds on his neck from her nails.

Calvin gasped and took a drink of water. "A simple no would have done fine," said Calvin indignantly. "Look, I'm just saying I'm shocked to hear your proposal. That's not traditionally how a woman acts, at least in my experience. Oh, and by the way, my answer is yes."

Tarpa looked a little puzzled. She squinted her eyes slightly and said, "Oh, I wasn't really asking, but I'm glad you're on board. It's always easier when I don't have to hold the guy down."

"Check please!" called Calvin to the waitress. The waitress just gave him a blank look and continued to wait on the next table.

"You know I'm just kidding," explained Tarpa, who probably wasn't kidding. "Of course it's got to be mutual. And if either of us has a problem with it, then we just call it off—no harm, no foul."

"Hey, you don't have to twist my arm," replied Calvin.

About that time, the waitress came over to take their orders. Tarpa ordered a fillet of ostrich. Calvin ordered a steak, but only after relentlessly questioning the waitress on its origins.

"I want a steak. From a cow. You know what a cow is, right? Do you have cows here? I don't want kitten steak, or dolphin steak, or poodle steak. I want a steak from a cow—the animal that grazes in the pasture and goes moo. So no funny business, all right?"

The waitress looked Calvin up and down and said with a forced smile, "Of course sir. As luck would have it, the steak is on special tonight and comes with a side of scalding hot coffee. How would you like that served, poured down your lap or dumped over your head?"

Calvin blinked. "I'll just have the steak, thank you." He slouched down in his chair slightly.

The waitress spun on her heals and left. Tarpa turned her attention back to Calvin and said, "Oh yeah, now I remember why I like you."

Calvin smirked. He wondered briefly why he liked Tarpa back, and then a thought struck him. "Hey," he said, "I saw the craziest feed earlier today."

"Oh yeah, of what?"

"I have no idea," explained Calvin.

"Sounds great."

"No, listen," continued Calvin, "it was of this woman tied up in a basement being force-fed cat shit while being clawed to death by kittens."

After a shock-filled pause, Tarpa replied, "Wow, that's crazy! Sounds like her cats had something against her. So, what made you bring that up? It's not exactly polite dinner conversation."

Calvin shrugged. "I don't know," he answered. "I was thinking of why I liked you, and somehow that feed sprung to mind."

Tarpa eyed him with suspicion. She was trying to figure out if Calvin knew that she was the mastermind behind that torture session, and whether or not it would be a bad thing if he did. She decided to go on the offense to throw him off his guard. She answered back, "I remind you of force-fed cat shit? Look, I can call off our deal if this is the way you are going to treat me."

Calvin stuttered a little while answering, "No, no that's not what I meant at all! I think it just reminded me a little of your second job. And I admire you for being strong willed enough to do that kind of work. Besides, I know that you would never do anything that sick to someone else. I mean, that was the work of a pure, deranged lunatic."

A little part of Tarpa was saddened by Calvin's reaction to her work. She considered the Kitty P. job to be her best work to date. And now here she was getting all emotional again. Damn him, she thought. I can't let him have that kind of sway over me. I already made up my mind that I'm not going to hide who I am anymore. She decided to confess to Calvin by saying, "A 65% robotic, deranged lunatic to be exact."

Calvin gaped. Calvin stared. He stuttered and whimpered. He wondered why God had to continually feed him carrots with one hand while beating him with a stick with the other.

Tarpa said nothing and bit her bottom lip. Finally Calvin cleared his throat a little and said, "Well, as long as you aren't a guy."

CHAPTER 14

Reunion

C alvin woke up in Room 7, which is something that he had sadly become accustomed to. He slowly sat up and rotated his feet off the side of the bed while stretching out his arms and arching his back. An exaggerated yawn escaped from his mouth as he scratched his stomach.

Calvin's hair was standing up like a mound of cotton candy and his face was stubbly. Normally this would not bother Calvin so much but since he now had a pseudo girlfriend he figured that he should try to maintain himself a little for her sake. With that thought in mind, Calvin stumbled into the bathroom, showered, and cleaned up his unruly follicles. He also used this time to take stock of his life.

Calvin was starting to reach a point of acceptance about his new life. He'd only had it, this life in the future, for about two weeks and a lot has happened to him in that short amount time. Now, though, he was beginning to realize that he had a nice place to stay and a job with flexible hours that he actually enjoyed. And he even had Tarpa's companionship to look forward to, so life was looking pretty good.

Tarpa. Calvin thought about her as he made his way to the door. He really liked her a lot despite her rather serious mental glitch of homicidal tendencies. He felt reasonably sure that he would never have to worry about her turning on him again as long as he did not mess with Ariel, which was easy enough to abide by. He loved Tarpa's smile, and he admired her strength and her frankness.

Calvin always had trouble dating overly sensitive woman because he inevitably ended up hurting them unintentionally and then resented being made to feel like the bad guy when most of the time his actions (or inactions) were completely without malice. He was clueless for sure, but he wasn't a bad man. Because of this, the idea of spending time with someone as thick-skinned as Tarpa was actually a major turn-on for Calvin.

And so for the first time in a while, Calvin felt serene. He was finally content with his current lifestyle and was hopefully optimistic about his future. This serenity, this hopeful optimism buzzed around Calvin's head as he made his way out of his room and into the hallway. It then reeled in horror and darted back inside the room leaving Calvin's head deserted while he tried to work out why his girlfriend from 300 years in the past was staring back at him with a look of blank incomprehension on her face.

A long couple of seconds passed before Calvin spoke. He managing to mumble, "Wha?"

His ex-girlfriend trumped him with a full word, "You."

Full words were still too much for Calvin, so he stuck with the basics, "Wha?"

His ex-girlfriend then dazzled him with, "Is it really?"

This sentence fragment gave Calvin enough time and enough of a voice sample to start solidifying his facts and form a reply which was this:

"Bianca?!?"

Bianca burst into tears. She leapt toward Calvin and threw her arms around him. Tears fell on Calvin's shoulder as Bianca whimpered, "It's you! It's really you. Calvin. I can't believe you're really here."

At that same time, Tarpa was around the corner with her own feeling of serenity and hopeful optimism buzzing around in her head, which promptly vanished when Tarpa rounded the corner and saw Calvin and Bianca hugging and kissing passionately. The small ember of warmth in Tarpa's soul that was struggling to become a fire was suddenly and painfully dashed out of existence by the joyful tears of the reunited couple, leaving only a tiny pile of soggy ash behind. Tarpa spun around and went back the way she had come.

The reunited couple gave each other a few more squeezes before disentangling from each other's embrace. Calvin, still a little dazed, started to seriously ask some questions, leading with the most obvious one.

"How are you here?"

Bianca tilted her head to one side slightly and said, "From what they tell me, I was frozen for some time. I was just revived three days ago. I thought you were gone, Calvin. I never, ever expected this, but I'm so glad." She gave him another quick hug.

Calvin hugged her back and said, "Me too, on both accounts. I was frozen too, only they brought me back about two weeks ago. I thought you were long gone, Bee." He sighed. "I can't tell you how awesome it is to see you again. I've been so alone and out of place here. This is so cool. I can't believe you're really alive. Now I have someone to share this bizarre new life with."

Bianca smiled. Calvin looked into her dark brown eyes and stared at the reflection of the hallway lights on their glossy surface. He was at a loss for words for a moment, but then another thought struck him and he asked, "So, wait. So you were frozen too. Does that mean that you also died, like me?"

Bianca felt a wave of nausea at the remembrance of that day, but she composed herself and answered, "Yes, Calvin, I died, just like you. On the very same day."

Calvin's face went "HUH?"

Bianca continued, "After you slammed down the phone during our conversation I thought you blew me off. I called back but I only got your voice mail, which made me even more angry. I left you a nasty message saying that I didn't want to see you anymore and I called you every name in the book."

"Wait, what? You broke up with me? I got in a car crash for Pete's sake. I was probably too busy bleeding on the side of the road to answer the phone." exclaimed Calvin.

"Well, I know that now," explained Bianca. "But how was I to know at the time? I thought you were mad at me. I thought you were ignoring me. That is, until later that night when I called to apologize but still couldn't reach you. I went around to your house but you weren't home. I called your Mom, looking for you. She was crying. She said you were in an accident." Bianca exhaled and looked down at the ground.

"I rushed to the hospital to see you. By the time I made it there, it was already too late." Bianca's voice crackled and she shook a little bit as she said, "You were already dead." She and Calvin both began to tear up and Bianca sniffled.

"They let me see you before they took you away. They gave me a little time alone with you. I thought of all the mean things I said to you on the answering machine. I couldn't believe that you were dead. I felt so horrible. I felt responsible. I couldn't face what I had done. I couldn't face a life without you. I didn't want to be alone. I had an old bottle of pain killers in my purse. I opened it and I swallowed down every one of the pills. I didn't want to feel the pain anymore. I didn't want to be without you. The last thing I remember was hugging you as the world became black."

Bianca hugged Calvin again, burying her face in his chest and soaking his shirt with tears. Calvin's face was resting on the top of her head as a stream of tears spilled down it and into Bianca's hair. He kissed the top of her head and said softly, "It's OK. It's OK. I'm here. We are together again. We are together. I'm here."

As Calvin stood there holding Bianca, his feelings of serenity and hopeful optimism peeked their cowardly heads out of Room 7, looked around cautiously, and tiptoed their way back into Calvin's subconscious. Calvin smiled a big, broad smile and gave Bianca a soft kiss.

CHAPTER 15

Scorned

Tarpa took the next available shuttle to Earth, and away from that "no good son of a bitch", which is something that she kept muttering under her breath during the majority of the trip.

I should have just stuck with my resolution, she thought. I was going to bury myself in my work, put all my energy into my craft and forget about that jerk from the stupid ages. But guess what, you no good son of a bitch, I have two jobs and one of them is to break you—brutally, repeatedly, and scientifically. Oh, and I'm going to do it all right. You'll see, you insensitive jerk, I'll mop the floor with you, and I'll do it with a smile.

She left the shuttle and entered the airport in search of the nearest ODIN entrance and was then almost tripped by her baggage as it sprinted across her path to join up with her. She took a swipe at it with her arm-knife but it dodged the attack, which made her even angrier. She gave it a surprise kick from behind and sent it flying over a railing. It made a graceful arc as it traveled down to the first floor where it smashed open causing a cloud of feminine clothing to rain down on a nearby elderly gentleman. He grinned. His wife swatted him with her purse, ostensibly to knock off the silky undergarments that were strewn about his person. "Don't you go gettin' no funny ideas mister," she said as one of the blows connected with his shoulder. The old man shook off a brassiere that was hanging off his head, and sighed.

Tarpa ignored all of this and went straight for the ODIN tunnels. She jumped into an empty capsule which began to take her home. As she traveled, she put her mind to use by thinking of the next experiment to test the limits of Calvin's healing ability. She considered some of the possibilities. She'd already broken his bones, and they seemed to heal up just fine. What could she try next? Fire? Drowning? Hazardous chemicals? Radiation? There are just so many choices, she thought with a smile. Maybe a flesh-eating virus; that would be fun. I wonder if I still have that Zaire Ebola virus sample? She reflected on this. Mmm, maybe a bad idea. But fire is a good start. Let's give that no-good bastard a chance to test out his new modifications.

CHAPTER 16

Modified

Calvin saw fuzzy, white light. After a while, the light focused to a point. He lay there squinting at it for some time before it was eclipsed by a face with long, black hair that draped down from it and tickled Calvin's nose. The face was feminine, warm, and serenely smiling at him. A soft voice asked, "How are you feeling, Cal?"

"I'm home," said Calvin. "I'm back. It was all just a sick dream." Calvin's face was coming alive.

"Cal, you're not home, you're at Bobcorp3."

Calvin's face dropped again.

"But how are you here?" he asked.

"Baby. Sweetie. I think you're still a little loopy from the anesthesia. Don't you remember? We re-united yesterday. Don't tell me you forgot last night," she said with a smirk.

Deep inside Calvin's brain a few synapses managed to rally together and fire a few times despite being suppressed by the residual anesthesia. "Oh," he said. "OH!" he repeated with feeling. He smiled a stupidly wide grin. "No, I remember last night alright."

Calvin looked around the familiar starkness of Room 7 and sighed. "You know, I spend so much time here I think I may have to decorate this place a little. Maybe some pictures over there, and a couch over there," he said while pointing at the back corner of the room. When he did this his arm shot with pain so he stopped doing it.

"Can't they send us back to our own time or something?" asked Calvin, more or less rhetorically.

"Well, if they freeze us, we'd just end up further in the future," replied Bianca, factually.

"Yes, but maybe like, if they freeze us long enough then time will loop back around and take us to our own time again."

Bianca shook her head. "I don't think that's going to happen, you goofball. Still," she said while looking around, "it doesn't seem too bad here. I really can't wait to see the Earth. From what you tell me, it sounds amazing. I think we will be just fine here. I think we'll be all right."

Calvin shrugged, which caused him a lot of pain so he stopped doing it.

About that time Bobford3 came through the door. "So, how's our little ice-pop doing today?" he asked the room.

"Hey Bob," replied Calvin. He groaned as he sat himself up. "I guess I'm not in bad shape for the shape I'm in," he said with a half-smile. "I'm pretty sore, but at least it seems like everything still functions."

"And how about you, sweet cheeks?" said Bobford3, addressing Bianca.

"I'm feeling pretty good, actually." She looked at Calvin and added, "As long as this one gets better soon, I really couldn't ask for anything else."

Bobford3 looked back at Calvin and said, "Man, Zero, I see you in a whole new light now. I mean, you're a good guy, don't get me wrong, but," he gestured toward Bianca, "I can't believe you got someone like her. Pretty, kind, and just the right amount of stupid."

Bianca playfully threw a pillow at Bobford3, which he allowed to bounce off of his face.

Calvin replied, "I'm definitely lucky on that account." He groaned. "Still, life always seems to balance out. I think I've paid my dues. I won't say I deserve her, but I do think the big guy upstairs felt he owed me a little something and took pity on me when he paired us up."

Bobford3 walked over to Calvin and handed him a glass. "Here you go, sport. Your favorite unnaturally orange breakfast drink slash industrial cleaner."

"You're still drinking Tang!" interrupted Bianca in disbelief. "I thought I told you that stuff will kill you."

Bobford3 interrupted right back, "Actually, sweet cheeks, Calvin is here today because of Tang." He looked her up and down. "And come to think of it, you are too. You must have done quite a bit of Tang swilling yourself there, missy. You have the same Tang effect as old mutant cells over there."

"Well, I mean, it's all he ever had in the fridge when I'd come to visit. What's this Tang effect thing?" inquired Bianca with a head-tilt.

"The Tang effect, as far as we can understand, is a genetic mutation which occurs as a result of the body's cells being bombarded with xanthan and cellulose gums in the presence of Yellow 6 coloring."

Bianca tilted her head a little more.

Bobford3, seeing this, felt the need to elaborate. "There is some stuff in Tang that modifies the genes of the cells. It causes them to gain a high-strength resin coating which preserves them almost like the wrapping of a mummy. This coating kept the cells intact through the freezing process. It also allows Calvin, and probably you as well, to heal at an extraordinary rate with the help of our nano-tech and a good, hardy dose of Tang."

Bianca looked doubtful.

"I'm serious; it's true," said Bobford3 before turning to Calvin. "Show her, Zero. We just sliced up most of your body to add your electro-muscular implants and your liquid nitrogen sprayer. Show Bianca your arm."

Calvin took his right arm back out from underneath the covers. He had a big, gnarly incision running down the length of it.

Bobford3 explained, "We normally do a better job of seaming things up, but there is no need to bother with old Zero Calvin over there. Go ahead Calvin, drink down the Tang."

Calvin was a little bothered that they were so careless with his body. He peered disdainfully at Bobford3 for a second and then gulped down the Tang.

Everyone stared at Calvin's arm with extreme focus. Calvin started to unconsciously hum the theme to Jeopardy until Bianca swatted him and told him to stop.

"Nothing's happening," stated Bianca.

"Just keep watching," replied Bobford3. "You have to be patient. It helps if you close your eyes for about twenty seconds and then open them again; then you'll see the small changes."

Bianca tried this. "Oh," she said. "I think I see it."

The worlds slowest freak show progressed for another ten minutes or so until the last few remnants of the surgery had disappeared.

Calvin moved his body around experimentally. He pulled back the covers and gave the rest of his body an appraisal. "I feel freaking awesome," exclaimed Calvin. He leapt out of bed and started doing a stupid little dance beside it.

Bianca looked at Bobford3 and said, "Wow, that's awesome. It's just a shame it didn't work on his brain."

"I know, right?!?" agreed Bobford3.

Calvin stopped dancing and lay back on the bed, looking betrayed. Bianca went back over to him, gave him a peck on the mouth, and then said, "I'm just kidding, goofy." She grinned, and so did Bobford3.

"Don't encourage her," he said while pointing at Bobford3. He then pointed at Bianca and said, "And you don't encourage him. I get enough abuse around here without your aid. You're supposed to be on my side, anyway. There's no 'I' in team but there is an 'M' and an 'E', so treat ME with respect."

Bianca was going to trash Calvin's wacko argument but decided instead to use it as a foot-in-the-door to bring up something else. "So we're a team, are we?"

"Of course," said Calvin. "We're together again, aren't we?"

Bianca took this and ran. "So we should probably live together then, right?"

"Excuse me," said Bobford3, "I'll just be dipping out now." He had already seen Bianca cry once before and he wasn't looking forward to hearing that shrill noise again.

Calvin quickly answered them both, "No, it's cool Bob; there's no problem here." He turned to Bianca. "Bee, of course we'll live together. I know that I've resisted in the past, but I've changed a lot in the last 300 years. Seriously, though, this world is kind of crazy and I want to make sure that you stay close by my side. I'm not into losing you again. Of course we'll live together."

Bianca gave him a huge hug and a kiss. Bobford3 saw this and felt the need to spoil the moment by saying, "Oh, now I see how you got a great girl like her—you're a sucker!"

Calvin was unperturbed by Bobford3's snide comment because he was too busy flashing back to some of the highlights of the night before as Bianca was kissing his neck. "Yes, maybe so Bob, but it's sooo worth it."

CHAPTER 17

Run!

Calvin was still in Room 7, convalescing. Bianca and Bobford3 had been gone for a few hours and Calvin was becoming incredibly bored. He bounced randomly from feed to feed looking for something decent to watch. On a whim, he switched to the Evionia feed.

What the hell are they doing now, Calvin asked himself. He was watching the two mullet-wearing guys that he had seen before . . . or was it? No, he thought, these are two new guys. What are they up to?

One of the guys was removing a make-shift balloon from a tube that led from what looked like an outhouse. He was wearing several layers of clothes and a makeshift helmet. The balloon he was holding looked off-white, like the color of natural rubber or latex, and it contained roughly one square foot of air, gas, or whatever was in it.

The other guy was messing with a pipe that had a short, stubby handle on it which made it look like a gun. In fact, it had a trigger mechanism on it as well, so Calvin guessed correctly that it was, in fact, some sort of primitive gun. The guy with the gun gave the trigger a few test squeezes. Each time it resulted in a flint spark inside the barrel, which could be seen from the outside through small air holes toward the back of the gun.

The guy holding the balloon handed it to the one with the gun, who promptly fastened it to the bottom of the handle. He took a potato from a sack that was slung over his shoulder and dropped it on the ground. Then he pushed the barrel of the gun through the potato, leaving a hole in the potato and a makeshift bullet wedged in the pipe.

"OK, run!" he said and then started counting to ten. The guy without the gun sprinted out into the field.

". . . eight, nine, ten!" said the gun holder. He ran out into the field in pursuit of his friend. After getting within ten meters of his friend, who was now bobbing and weaving in the wheat field, he took aim and pulled the trigger.—FOOM!—PANK—

He scored a direct hit to his friend's head. He yelled out, "32 to 18, I win again!" His friend had already taken off his helmet and was rubbing his head.

Calvin looked completely despondent. He shook his head and went back to flipping through the feeds. About that time Tarpa came in the room with lunch for Calvin.

"How are you feeling, sport?"

Calvin's mind snapped back into the real world and his eyes focused on Tarpa. "Oh, hi. I didn't notice you coming in. Um, I'm doing fine. I feel great. Do you think I'll be able to go back home soon?"

Tarpa put the tray of sandwiches on the nightstand next to Calvin's bed and handed him a sandwich. "Oh yes," she responded, "You're just fine. You can go home shortly and can resume work immediately." She gave Calvin a mischievous little smirk and added, "The sooner, the better, in fact."

"Why is that?" he asked, noticing the smirk.

"No reason," answered Tarpa with a shrug. "I just figured that the sooner you get back to work the sooner you can get back to earning karma. I'd hate for you to go negative—then I'd be forced to visit you for something other than quality time." She ended this with a forced laugh.

Calvin was getting a little nervous. He rubbed the back of his head and began stammering a reply, "Ah, yes, about that. I think I'm going to have to sort of, well, call off our deal. You see, I . . ."

"I know," interrupted Tarpa, flatly. "It's cool. I know you're back with your ex. It's OK. It was a bad idea of mine anyway; I'd just be wasting my time with you just like Ariel says."

Calvin was confused, mad, and relieved all at once. He wasn't sure how to answer. He figured she was probably hurt and was covering it up by lashing out, so he decided to just let the insult slide. "OK, well, I'm sorry just the same. I know you are kind of lonely. I still hope we can hang out as friends. Bianca gets a little jealous sometimes, but she'll just have to deal with it."

"What am I just going to have to deal with?" asked Bianca, who had just walked in on the tail-end of their conversation.

The look of shock and horror on Calvin's face was one for the record books. All he wanted to do was to show a little loyalty toward Tarpa to make her feel better, but as always, his good intentions came back to haunt him. He snapped to attention and began stammering like the dumb ass that he was. "Oh, well, um, hi sweetie. I was just saying to, um, Tarpa here that I, I mean, um, Tarpa and I should, you know, um, finish our game of Myst some time or whatever but I was afraid that maybe, um, you know, you get sort of jealous sometimes—which I don't mind—and, well, that's it really."

Bianca switched to her cross-examiner's disposition. "Should I be jealous, Calvin? Do you two have some sort of history together?"

Calvin looked over at Tarpa. "No, no, nothing really. I mean we never dated or anything. She's just the first person I met here and we hang out sometimes, is all."

Tarpa saw clearly where Calvin's true allegiance was. She stood up and started walking toward the door. As she left, she said with her back to the two of them, "Excuse me, I have to get back to work. Don't worry about it Bianca, I don't think Calvin and I are going to be seeing much of each other outside of this place anymore." With that, she left the room.

This really hurt Calvin and he wanted to smooth things over with Tarpa but he couldn't because then Bianca would get the wrong impression. He tried to act as if he wasn't worried at all that Tarpa seemed to be mad at him. He grabbed Bianca's hand and said to her, "She's very busy. She has two jobs, you know.

Not much time left for playing games with me. But anyway, like I said, you don't have to worry about me and her; we never hooked up even when you were not here. We're not interested in each other that way. We were just two lonely people killing time."

"It's OK, Calvin, I trust you. And besides, Ariel would rat you out in a heartbeat if you ever cheated on me. Ariel is my friend; she tells me things. She tells me everything. She's like my big sister, always looking out for me. I don't have to worry about you or anything else as long as I have her."

"Oh, well, that's good," replied Calvin. "Just the same, even without Ariel you still don't have anything to worry about. We are together, we are a team. That means a lot to me, and I will never do anything to screw that up. My loyalty is with you. I'm sorry for the jealousy wisecrack, you weren't meant to hear that. I was just trying to reassure Tarpa that we will still hang out because she is a lonely person and I knew she was worried that me having a girlfriend would prevent us from hanging out anymore. It was a dick thing to say about you, but like I said I was trying to make her feel better. She's a little rough on the outside, but she is fragile just like anyone. Please, I don't want this to be an issue with us."

"Enough, Cal. I told you, it's fine. I'm not worried. Just forget about it. I promised myself that it wasn't going to be like before. I'm not going to let petty things upset me. Ariel helped me to realize that you can't dwell on what might happen in the future, the same as you can't waste your time dwelling on the past. The best thing to do is to enjoy the present, and gently steer it toward a better tomorrow."

"Wow," said Calvin, "Ariel never tells me good stuff like that. She usually just tells me that she is 100% operational and then insults me. Now I'm kind of jealous."

Bianca chuckled. "Well, you did try to hack her brain."

Calvin's award winning shock-face assembled itself again. "She told you that?"

"Oh yes," answered Bianca factually. She stared into his eyes and then said calmly, "And she told me why."

There it was, that hall of fame shock-and-horror face in all its glory. Calvin was absolutely horrible at keeping his composure. His face was easier to read than a children's book. His brain lurched. It sat quivering in the back corner of his head and shook like a scared puppy. Calvin was doing a quick mental recall of what he had told Bianca about Tarpa and compared it to this new information. His brain whimpered and wet itself. Calvin's mouth opened and closed but nothing was coming out.

Bianca gave him a nice calm smile. It was hard to tell if she was glad she had caught him in a lie, or if she was genuinely OK with the situation. Calvin was guessing it was the former. Bianca, smiling, said, "It's OK, I told you, I'm not going to let silly things get to me."

Calvin's brain finally had something to say. It scribbled it down hastily on a napkin and handed it to his mouth. His mouth read it aloud, "That was way in the beginning. I was lonely, and besides she killed me after that so I don't like her so much anymore."

"Calvin!"

"What?"

"It's OK. Honestly, it's OK. Just be straight with me from now on, right? I understand. You were just trying to appease me. I'm trying hard not to be as fragile as I used to be. I want to be the kind of person you can share anything with. So please, from now on, have faith in me. No more secrets."

Calvin looked down at the bed. "Bob was right. I really don't deserve you."

Bianca rested her hand on his head and said, "Just remember that and I think we will get along just fine." She gave him a gentle hug. "Why don't you get yourself together and we'll head back to Earth today." She saw the half-drank glass of tang on the nightstand and asked, "Mind if I have the rest of that? I'm dying of thirst."

"Of course. Be my guest."

Bianca held the glass high and said, "Well, here's to our common past and our hopeful future." With that she gulped it down as fast as she could and then screwed up her face. "Blah! This stuff is as harsh as ever."

"Hey!" said Calvin, "Show Tang some respect. It's like a holy drink to me—to us. It's why we're able to be together right now."

Bianca said with her face still puckered, "Maybe so, but it really is dreadful." She started to smile, but a sharp pain in her head caused it to contort into a scowl. Her world went swimmy and she sat heavily onto Calvin's bedside and clenched her head with both hands.

"You OK?" asked Calvin as he sat up and grabbed hold of her shoulders."

Bianca didn't answer right away, but after about twenty worrying seconds the pain and dizziness subsided and she slowly returned to her normal self. Finally, she answered, "Yes, sorry, I'm OK. I just got like a massive headache all the sudden. Maybe it was just brain-freeze from drinking the cold Tang too fast."

Calving relaxed a bit and answered, "Don't freak me out like that. I thought you were really sick."

"No, sorry, I'm OK now." She pinched the bridge of her nose for a second and then opened her eyes back up and looked at Calvin. "That really is horrible stuff."

CHAPTER 18

Fire!

It was a beautiful Tuesday afternoon in Newark but Bianca wanted nothing to do with it. She had been in bed, hiding under the covers now for about an hour and she was determined to stay there until Calvin returned from work.

The moon buggy ride to the shuttle had almost made her puke and the shuttle's takeoff had succeeded. And just when she had thought that the nightmarish travel was over, Calvin had put her in a tube which somehow dropped out of the sky even though it started from the inside of a building. There had been vomit involved in this as well. The only slightly good thing was that Calvin had thoughtfully given her his extra air-sickness bag and some Listerine pills. Calvin had tried to prepare Bianca for these experiences but the anticipation of it all only made it worse for her. Bianca was not a happy traveler.

After they had made it back to their apartment and Calvin had shown her around, Bianca decided that she wasn't really feeling up to sightseeing just yet. She wasn't "in the right frame of mind for it" as she had said.

She had told Calvin to go ahead and do what he needed to do today. She was just going to take a little nap. With that, Calvin had decided to go to work since he felt that Tarpa was trying to hint that he needed some more karma.

Shortly after Calvin had left, Bianca heard some rustling around in the apartment and wearily went to investigate. A giant mechanical robot jumped out and tried to be friends with her. The shrill yell of horror and a racing pulse rate were enough signs for Ariel to intervene and send the cleaning robot back to its lair.

And so Bianca was now steadfastly planted under the covers and she wasn't coming out until Calvin returned home, or possibly ever. To make matters worse, she was having occasional headaches and dizzy spells similar to the one earlier in the day, only not quite as severe. She was also starting to see things, or rather, imagine things. Odd dream-like visions would flicker into her mind of places and things she had never seen before.

She thought about Calvin and wondered what he was doing right now. Calvin had explained that he was a park ranger of sorts. She thought that that was a vague and shifty explanation and was quite interested in what he actually did all day.

She thought about Calvin walking in the park and a vivid view of it appeared in her mind. She was walking just behind Calvin now, almost like she had entered the body of a stranger. She looked around and could see the park-like city with its multicolored walkways and its oddly-shaped building off in the distance.

Bianca continued to follow Calvin as he walked his territory. They passed a couple of pretty college girls and Calvin turned around and looked at their butts as they walked away. They were wearing skirts with a college emblem printed on the back—NSU. Instinctively, Bianca ran up and tried to smack Calvin on the head, but she failed miserably because she wasn't really there and only succeeded in swatting her pillow off the bed.

As Calvin continued to walk the route, the crowd started to thin out a little. Bianca was finding it hard to look where she wanted sometimes, which was really getting on her nerves. As the crowd thinned more, her view started to jump around to different perspectives, some walking toward Calvin, some from behind, and occasionally one from odd places as if she were sitting on a pole or up in a tree. This was really annoying her.

Calvin was alerted by Ariel of a wildfire off to the left, about 200 meters into the woods. Calvin darted into the woods to investigate, skillfully negotiating shrubs, vines, tree branches, and sticker patches. Bianca lost sight of Calvin and was unable to look in any direction but straight. She wondered what he was up to, darting off into the woods like that.

As she was wondering that, her perspective shifted again. Suddenly she was being hurtled through the woods with reckless abandon. She could hear heavy breathing and could see hands and feet whisking vegetation out of the way and sprinting over the torturous topography. She thought she could make out smoke off in the distance.

Calvin quickly arrived at the source of the smoke, which not surprisingly was a fire. It was spreading fast in the dry summer underbrush so Calvin had little time to waste. Bianca heard Calvin's voice as he said, "Well, here goes nothing." She watched through his eyes as Calvin pointed his right arm at the thickest part of the fire. A mist of liquid nitrogen sprayed from a nozzle just behind the back of his wrist. He moved his arm in large sweeping movements as he aimed for the base of the fire and in short time the fire was almost completely extinguished. Unfortunately, so was Calvin's nitrogen supply so he had to switch tactics and kick dirt at the last remnants of the flames and jump on top of them, stamping them out.

This proved to be very difficult to do because the fire seemed to have several ignition points. As Calvin would stamp out one area, another would flare up behind him. It was just within his abilities to get it under control, but eventually he did.

Calvin's feet and legs were burned and he was exhausted. He stood still for a moment and caught his breath, choking on the smoke in the air.

Bianca heard a loud pop from behind them. Calvin also noticed it and spun around in time to see a tree heading his way. The fire had apparently weakened the trunk. Bianca screamed at Calvin to move but this had no effect since she wasn't really there.

The tree was towering over them now and moving fast. Bianca heard Calvin mumble, "Here goes nothing—again." Calvin raised his arms up in the air and braced for the impact. Compared to the bulk of the tree, Calvin's arms looked like twigs from a sapling. Bianca tried to close her eyes but they were already closed. She could do nothing but watch as this bizarre dream continued.

—SMACK—HUMPH!—

Bianca couldn't see it, but Calvin was grinning like a mental patient just after medicine time. He was fine. He was more than fine. He was holding up one side of a tree that must have been several hundred pounds.

"You're not getting the best of me again you stupid tree," shouted Calvin as he shoved it safely away from him. Bianca watched as Calvin held his hands in front of him and stared at his palms. They were red and his hands were shaking, but they were fine. Bianca could hear heavy breathing and could almost sense the adrenaline surging around in Calvin's body with no useful destination. Calvin sat down on top of the fallen tree. He was the conqueror, but he felt conquered. He grabbed a bottle of tang from his backpack, took a long pull from it, and sighed.

Back in the apartment, Bianca also felt exhausted and collapsed under the covers where she slept soundly for the next few hours.

—THUNK—

What was that, thought Bianca as she was jolted out of her deep sleep. Could it be that that mechanical monster is running around the apartment again?

She mustered up her courage as she grabbed a nearby foot-tall bronze statue of Godzilla that Calvin had obtained recently as a decoration for his room. She sprung out of the bedroom waving Godzilla around menacingly and shouted, "Get the fuck out of here you bastard!"

Calvin dove behind the island that separated the kitchen from the dining room. "What the fuck did I do?"

Bianca dropped the statue and ran over to Calvin while apologizing profusely.

"Sorry, sorry, sorry! I thought you were the big spider thing again. I'm sorry."

Calvin slowly stood back up. He looked at the living room and noticed that all of the furniture had been moved in front of the place in the wall in which the cleaning robot makes its dastardly appearance. "I see," said Calvin levelly. "Ariel!" said Calvin in a low grumble.

"Yes?" answered a ghostly voice in his head.

"You know when I said that that thing isn't allowed out when I'm home?"

"Affirmative."

"Well, change that. It isn't allowed out when anyone is home. Anyone at all."

"OK," answered Ariel simply.

Bianca interrupted, "Actually Ariel, just get rid of that damn thing. I'll do the cleaning. I don't want that thing living in my walls. I'll clean the apartment myself."

"OK," answered Ariel simply.

Calvin, who was now standing beside Bianca, put his arm around her, gave her a one-handed hug, and asked her, "Are you OK, Bee?"

"I'm fine now, Cal. How about you, are you OK?" Bianca said this as she was gently squeezing his arms and patting down his body.

"I'm fine, why?"

"Oh," she answered not knowing if she should explain herself or even if she could. "Um nothing. I just wanted to know if you had a rough day or an easy one."

Calvin took a breath. "Well, I guess it was a rough day. But it was a good day if that makes any sense."

Bianca shrugged.

"I had to put out a fire today and that went pretty well thanks to my new modifications. So that was tough but rewarding. But then, um—now I don't want you to worry, this kind of stuff doesn't usually happen—but, well, I almost got crushed by a tree today."

Bianca gasped. She was in shock. It hadn't been a dream. She really had been somehow riding shotgun with Calvin today.

Calvin misinterpreted the gasp and tried to calm her down. "It's OK! It's OK. I'm fine. I was able to save myself thanks to my mods. So you see, it was a tough day, but it was also a good day. Because, you know, I didn't die or anything," he said with a weak smile.

So this was all real, thought Bianca. Calvin really did almost die today. She gasped again at this realization and swung a half-hearted right hook which connected with Calvin's shoulder and hurt him not at all. "You idiot! Don't be so reckless! You can't leave me again, you idiot!"

She started swinging again but Calvin muffled the blows by hugging her. He kissed the top of her head and said, "It's OK. I told you, we're together now. I'm not going anywhere. I'm pretty tough, you know. But I promise I'll be more careful from now on."

Bianca looked up at him with sad eyes and said, "You'd better." She buried her face in his chest and mumbled to herself, "I'll be watching you to make sure."

CHAPTER 19

Harem

"Thanks for meeting me here, Tarpa. I've been wanting to continue our game, but things have been a little hectic," explained Calvin as he removed his display lenses.

Tarpa took the cue from Calvin and removed hers as well. "Yes, well, you do have to babysit Little Miss Pukey. I hear she keeps you on a short leash."

"Don't call her that—she is my girlfriend you know. I wish you two could get along better," said Calvin

"Why is that, sport, you trying to start yourself a little harem? I hear Evianna in Logistics has been putting the moves on you too. You're quite the popular one, aren't you Zero?"

"Evianna? You mean that girl who says "Hello genius" and kicks me every time I come through the airlock door?"

"Yes, precisely. Her dedication is really quite charming, isn't it?" answered Tarpa with a smirk.

"More like psychotic. No, I think I'll have to pass on your harem idea. I have a hard enough time with Bianca alone."

"Why, what's up with her?"

"Nothing. I love her, and we're getting along great, but."

"But . . . ?"

"But man is she suspicious. I keep getting the feeling that she's watching me through Ariel somehow. Sometimes she makes little snide comments about something, and then I realize that she could only know it if she were watching me at work. I really love her, but I think this will spoil things between us if it keeps up."

Tarpa nonchalantly inspected her nails and replied, "Maybe that's just your guilty conscience speaking."

"I haven't done anything wrong," exclaimed Calvin.

"And yet here you are, sneaking around with me and talking about your girlfriend behind her back. Hmm," replied Tarpa while raising an eyebrow at Calvin.

"Alright, point taken. But you know we aren't doing anything bad."

"You know that and I know that, but she wants to be sure of that. I think it's fine, Calvin. That sort of behavior happens from time to time. After a while, it will settle down. But you really should be mindful of how things look, Calvin. Because even if Bianca stops actively watching you, Ariel is sure to keep monitoring you just as she does all of us. Cheating and disloyalty toward your partner will earn you some seriously negative karma."

Calvin shook his head. "I'm not worried about that. I am loyal to Bianca. I won't betray her, even with someone as charming as you." He rolled his eyes. "But I do have loyalty to you too, you know. You're the only friend I have here. I can relax around you. I think you know me pretty well, even my faults, and you accept me. And although I don't know a lot about you, what I do know I accept. So I'm glad we are here together today regardless of how Bianca sees it, because I love my time spent with you and I look forward to getting to know you even better."

Tarpa was caught off guard. She suddenly thought about the experiments that she has been doing on Calvin and about the ones that she still had to do, and felt a tightness in her chest. She reached out and gave Calvin a hug and spoke in his ear, "We better put our glasses back on. I'm sure Miss Pukey thinks we are bumping uglies right now. I don't want my friend to get into trouble." She gave him a kiss on the cheek.

Calvin actually blushed. It was cute. "OK," he said while trying to pull himself together, "let's get back into this game." He pulled his lenses out of his pocket, blew off some pocket fluff, and clicked them into place. Tarpa removed hers from a lint-free compartment in her left arm and put them on as well.

The last time they were in Myst Village, Calvin and Tarpa spent four and a half hours walking around a mountain to get their first clue, which was this: 'WEST'. So they made their way back to their last save point and headed west, as best they could judge by the angle of the artificial two o'clock sun. Before too long, they came up to a deep fissure in the ground that was too wide to jump. Tarpa offered to throw Calvin across, but he declined. So the pair of them followed the fissure north because they thought they saw a bridge maybe a kilometer away. A short, shaggy, old man seemingly sprang out of thin air and blocked the path to the bridge.

Calvin laughed. "Let me guess, you're going to ask us three questions that we must answer correctly before we can cross the bridge like 'What is our favorite color?' and 'What is the average airspeed velocity of an unladen swallow?'"

"Oh no, no, no, muttered the old man. I think that comes later on in the game. I'm just here to tell you to watch your step. The bridge is wet from the rain last night and it's as slippery as an oiled eel. You've been warned." The old man hobbled away from them muttering, "Snotty little kid," and then he puffed out of existence.

Tarpa smiled. "At least he didn't kick you in the shins and call you a genius."

"Oh come on," pleaded Calvin, "don't tell me that didn't look a little Monty Pythonish to you."

"I've never seen it."

"Oh. Oh? Oh, come on now, sister, you haven't even lived yet if you haven't seen anything from Monty Python. Tonight we'll have movie night and we are totally watching *The Quest for the Holy Grail*. I think it will fit in nicely with," Calvin gestured around him with his hands, "all of this. Anyway, come along." He reached down and grabbed Tarpa's hand. "Watch your step. I hear it is as slippery as an eel's ass out there."

The two of them crossed the bridge without incident and continued to walk and talk. "So, tell me. How did you get started doing your . . . other job? What was your first time like? Scary? Fun? What?" probed Calvin.

"Well, I was pretty young when they identified me; I think I was maybe eleven. I didn't really have any friends growing up, not that I really have many now either. I wasn't by any stretch mean, just not very friendly. Or, actually, I guess you could say I was withdrawn. I never really cried or laughed like the other kids, so I guess I spooked them out a little. As time went by, I learned to mimic their emotional behavior better and so things eventually became easier for me. I learned what responses were expected of me and soon, by sheer repetition, they became a habit.

"The adults, and of course Ariel, saw that I had a unique brain and decided that it was best put to use in learning to be a Dark Angel. That's what they call us—that or Karma Police. Personally, I prefer Dark Angel—at least it sounds sexy."

"Um, yeah, I agree. Dark Angel isn't bad," agreed Calvin. He continued, "So, let me get this straight. You taught yourself to have emotions?"

Tarpa shook her head. "No, of course not. Emotions are just there, you can't learn them. What I learned to do was to mimic them. My emotions are nothing but hard logic. I evaluate the situation that I'm in, decide from past observation what emotional display is best suited to it, and then carefully act it out. Of course, like I said, I no longer do it consciously. Everything happens automatically now, almost like I'm a normal person."

"I think you have real emotions now. OK, yes you tend to be cold and calculating, but I think you do have a capacity for emotions now, don't you? I mean, you're here with me now, right? I don't think you're here out of some pre-programmed sense of social normality. You're here because you want to be here, because walking around in the desert with me and watching me get insulted by magical old men actually makes you happy. And I think I've seen you sad before. And jealous. Face it sweetie, you are more than just a killing machine. You're human, just like me."

"Let's not get carried away, Calvin. I'm not so sure that you're human. You're like some sort of walking talking Tang monster, really. But thanks, I know what you're trying to say and I appreciate it. I think it is thanks to you that I am coming out of my shell. At first I was worried about it, and even resentful and frightened, but I've come to terms with it now and with your help I think I can cope."

Calvin said, "You make it sound like you've caught a disease from me."

Tarpa shrugged. "Well, kind of. Emotions are just these weird things that make you do irrational things. They mess up your decision-making abilities and make you weak. At least, that's what I thought a first. But now, maybe, I'm seeing that they can make you stronger too.

"But I do worry, Calvin. I worry that my emotions are going to interfere with my work. What if I start to feel sorry for someone I'm meant to terminate? What then? What if I start feeling guilt? I'm ashamed to say it, Calvin, but since we seem to be having some sort of therapy session, I might as well admit it. I need to kill people, Calvin. Need. If I don't do it every few days, I get edgy and anxious. You saw the kind of things I do, Calvin, like with that woman and her cats. I'm not normal Calvin, not by a long shot."

Calvin stopped walking, and since they were still absent-mindedly holding hands, Tarpa was brought up short. "It's OK, Tarpa. It's OK." Calvin sighed. "I'll put it to you this way: you might need to kill, but you choose to only kill people who deserve it. As far as I know, you've never killed out of jealousy or rage or whatever. Even if it bothers you, you can wait and do the right thing. That makes you a good person. You're not a normal person, but you are a good person."

Tarpa bit her bottom lip and shook her head. "No, don't you see, that's just it Calvin—I never killed out of anger or any other emotion because I didn't have them. But now I'm starting to. So now what? What if I get jealous of you and Miss Pukey and I cut her pretty little head off?"

"You wouldn't"

"Maybe I would. We don't know."

"I know. You wouldn't. Because where there are emotions there is empathy. You wouldn't do it because you know it would ruin me, and the thought of that hurts you. Even if you really are the monster that you paint yourself to be, you still have a steel-trap mind when it comes to logic and reason. You wouldn't kill her because you know it would make me hate you, and therefore, it would not work as a way of getting closer to me but quite the opposite." Calvin paused for thought. "And don't call her Miss Pukey; I told you not to be mean to her. She's my girlfriend and I love her. So no cutting her head off, you hear me?"

"Yeah, I hear you. And Calvin . . . thanks. I actually feel a little better now." Tarpa looked around and continued, "You know, I don't think I feel like playing this any more today. How about we go somewhere and watch that Monty thingy you were blabbing on about?"

Calvin agreed. He looked down at their hands, still joined together. Tarpa followed his gaze and they both let go a little guiltily. Tarpa looked at him sideways. "Are you sure you're not trying to start a harem?"

CHAPTER 20

Distractions

Every city, no matter how clean, futuristic, and advanced it might be, has a shady downtown area. This is an irrevocable fact of the universe. This is because the universe is a bewildering cesspool of random chaos and human beings stupidly try to tidy it up into something they call reality. This spawns the need for humans to insulate themselves from the chaos in one of two ways: 1) They invent a god and assign him/her/it the responsibility of sorting out the mess, then they tell themselves that they can't know the mind of god so they won't always know why something happens but they must have faith that god is taking care of it all. 2) They accept the world for what it is and drink a lot to cope with it.

In the hyper-technological age in which Bianca now finds herself, science and statistics have proved that the actions assigned to every major god fall within the margins of random chance, thus removing any hope of anyone living their life with their head comfortably buried in the sand. So, as Bianca wandered through the entertainment district of Newark, she found the place to be alive with distractions. If Mardi Gras could take on human form and have sex with a sky diver on cocaine, the offspring would be downtown Newark, also known as Little Akiba. And this was only Thursday. You should see the place on the weekend. Actually, on second thought you shouldn't—not without a welder's helmet or you would go blind. Bianca thought it might be fun.

She dipped into a bar suitably named "Distractions". A burst of flame shot out in front of her as she entered. A sheepish looking man in a suit wiped his mouth and said, "Oh sorry love, didn't see you there." The barman put a glass down heavily on the bar top and shouted over at the man in the suit and his fellow colleagues, "Oi! You blokes wander off to the back room, K?" One of them belched a small flame and a puff of smoke, which gently singed the hair on the back of someone's head. "Like now!" the barman added.

Bianca pushed pass the gentlemen and made her way to the bar. As she sat down, she noticed an advert for a special event. It read "Thursday, April 24th—Businessman's Flamethrower Contest. Get into the *spirit!* It's an *Absolute* must!" She shook her head and stood back up while muttering to herself, "On second thought, I don't think I'm quite ready for this level of entertainment," and quickly left the bar.

"Oi!" shouted the barman, "See what you guys did. You chased away another lovely. That's the third one today. Now get your asses in the back before I kick 'em there."

Bianca went back to her sightseeing tour of downtown Newark. The place definitely had a carnival feel to it. Several booths, shops, and bars littered the landscape as if a giant child had just had a temper tantrum and had thrown his Lego blocks around the city in protest of some unknown injustice, most likely an early bedtime. In contrast to the city proper, downtown was much more organic in layout, random but not chaotic, bustling but friendly. Interesting and busy is the sort of idea we are going for here. It was not so much planned by a community as it was the cumulative result of thousands of individuals spotting a plot of land and saying to themselves, "Yeah, that'll do."

Bianca looked around wildly, trying to soak in just one tenth of the madness that was going on around her: an electric chair chess competition (the timer was programmed to shock you if you didn't make your move in time), a cardion craft expo, a laser tag maze with real 40W lasers, a modder's expo (sort of a beauty pageant, sort of a freak show in which the participants show off their body mods), a roof runner's competition (a race from one end of town to the other, jumping only from rooftop to rooftop), the hobbyist geneticist's showcase (oh my, you can't imagine the animals), a liquid mercury swimming pool and detox salon, an oobleck diver's competition, a DIY rocket pack center, and a bingo table (for the elderly). And that's just what she could see from her spot in front of the bar.

She watched in blank incomprehension as a roof jumper got distracted in mid jump by a stray laser beam from the laser tag game, which burnt a small divot in his right leg. His jump ended up short and he bounced off the wall of the opposite building, fell, and splashed down into the liquid mercury pool below. Liquid mercury splashed into the air and into the eyes of a novice aviator who was wearing a rocket pack that he had cobbled together out of metal piping and sausages. The aviator went out of control and swooped down onto the chess club, knocking over the timer which then electrocuted both players simultaneously. The giant mutant canary bird that had just won first prize at the geneticist's showcase became overly excited by the rocket man that had just whizzed over its head. It broke free of its shackles and pursued him. An oobleck diver narrowly missed a collision with the runaway rocket man, but instead landed on the back of the giant canary. The canary freaked out and flew upside down to dump its unwanted cargo. The oobleck diver flailed helplessly as he plummeted into the middle of a young girl's demonstration of her spring-loaded leg kick, which sent him flying toward the courtyard next door. He crash landed on the one and only bingo table in the entire city and was severely beaten by cross old ladies with crutches and handbags. Meanwhile, the rocket man ran out of sausage power and dropped out of the sky like, well, like a human without lift. He was right over the cardion expo and could do nothing to prevent the inevitable pain of landing on top of a Gothic cathedral modeled from pure cardion (which was very, very pretty, but very, very spiky). Just before he was to be impaled by art, the canary swooped down and grabbed him with its massive talons. It flew off to some discrete location where it did unspeakable things to him which, well, we will not speak of.

Bianca blinked twice, turned, and ran to the nearest ODIN station. Later on that night, when Calvin asked her what she did all day, she could only just shrug and say, "Nothing much." She thought, how do I even begin to explain it?

CHAPTER 21

Electrodes

"Velcro really likes you," said Calvin in amazement. Bianca had just come home from shopping. Before she could even close the door behind her, Calvin's cat (now officially and aptly named Velcro) did a running turbo-kitty dive for Bianca's chest. Bianca had just caught it in her arms, triggering Calvin's observation.

"They say animals are a great judge of character," answered Bianca.

Calvin smirked. "Could be, could be. Or, it could be that you feed him every day."

Bianca gave Calvin a cold look.

"I'm just saying," added Calvin with his hands up. He walked over and gave Bianca a kiss. Velcro took a swipe at his chin but just missed as Calvin narrowly dodged the attack.

"See," said Bianca, "a great judge of character."

"Calvin eyed the cat up and down. "Traitor."

Velcro nuzzled itself into Bianca's chest and purred.

"Well, Whatever. Maybe I'll just get a big old dog. Dogs are loyal."

"And maybe," replied Bianca, "maybe you can sleep on the couch from now on." She winked and walked past him on the way to the ODIN delivery door in the dining room. She opened it up and retrieved her groceries.

"You're really getting the hang of this world, aren't you?" asked Calvin rhetorically.

"Yeah, well, it's been a couple of weeks already and everything is pretty easy. And if I don't know how to deal with something, Ariel shows me how—usually before I even ask. Like today, when I went to the grocery store, I just looked at the corn and before I knew it there was a robot there to collect it for me. It was dressed like a butler and talked all aristocratically. Too funny.

"Anyway, Jeeves followed me around the store—I named him Jeeves, how could I not—and all I had to do was THINK that I wanted something and Jeeves would collect it into his basket. And then when I was done, Jeeves said that he would send them to my place directly, madam. He called me madam! And then I walked back because it's so damn nice out and here I am. And here's the groceries. I love this place!"

"Nice," replied Calvin. "I'm glad you're doing OK. I guess I can thank Ariel for taking care of you. It seems you two have bonded, weirdly enough. So, what do you want to do today? I've got the day off, and you're basically a freeloader . . ."

"I just haven't figured out what to do yet," interjected Bianca.

"Ah, well, you know I'm just kidding around. Seriously, don't sweat it. As it stands, you are quite valuable to this society just by existing. I reckon that you're on the gravy train for life here. Don't worry about a thing. Now then, what did you want to do today?"

"I'm not too sure what there is to do here. I don't think I really want to loaf around on the beach—besides, I know how easily you burn and then get all cranky."

"I don't burn."

"Yeah, right, you're practically Italian. A blonde-headed, blue-eyed Italian."

"It just takes time."

Bianca chuckled, "Fine. Anyway, I'm truly not into the beach today. How about, oh, I don't know, maybe an amusement park? They have those here, right?"

"Well," said Calvin, "I know they have Myst Village, but I don't think it's your kind of place."

"Oh, you mean the place you take your girlfriend Tarpa to when you guys want to be alone?"

"Ha ha. Yes, that place. I mean no. I mean . . . you know what I mean. Anyway, I'll ask Ariel . . ."

"Already did. There are several of them within a half hour of here. I say we head for the one with the craziest coasters. It's called *The Screaming Skeleton*."

"I don't get you. You hate the moon rover, you hate the shuttle, you hate the ODIN tunnels, but you like roller coasters. Well, whatever, it sounds fun."

Bianca shrugged. "Actually, I quite like the tunnels now. As soon as I figured out how to see what was really going on, they are just like riding on a roller coaster, really. I'm fine with things on a track, but when it's something like the rover or the shuttle—all bumping and weaving all over—well, quite frankly, it makes me a little pukey."

On that lovely note, they decided to take a walk through the park-like city and catch an ODIN tunnel there so that they could enjoy the outdoors a bit. While they were walking, Bianca suddenly spun around and snatched a Frisbee from the air, a fraction of a second before it was to connect with the back of Calvin's head. Some amazed kids waved to Bianca. Calvin felt the air from the Frisbee and turned to see Bianca, who was throwing the Frisbee back and waving to the kids.

"What the? How'd you see that coming?"

"I don't know." She shrugged. "I just knew it was coming. Like a feeling. No, more than a feeling. I just knew it was coming—don't ask me how."

"You just knew it was coming," muttered Calvin, half to himself. "Weird. Cool, but weird."

Bianca replied, "Ariel just told me that she put the thought into my head to protect you."

"She can do that?"

"Apparently, but only with me. She and I are pretty close. It has something to do with me having special powers, or at least that's what Bob told me when I first got here."

"Bob—I should have known. I'm going to have to have a little chat with that crazy clone some time soon. But anyway, thanks for the save." Calvin looked up. "Oh, you too Ariel."

Ariel: You are welcome, Calvin.

Calvin nodded. "Me and Ariel, we're pretty tight too."

Bianca patted him on the shoulder with a grin. "Of course you are dear, of course you are."

They caught the next ODIN shuttle to the outskirts of town and arrived to the place known as The Screaming Skeleton.

The Screaming Skeleton was not so much an amusement park but a place were methamphetamine addicts go after they have burned out all of their dopamine receptors and therefore have to resort to going to a place where pleasure and excitement is delivered in nearly deadly proportions.

It wasn't the chaotic sort of fun that you got in the seedier parts of Newark like Little Akiba, but more like a scientifically distilled, precisely delivered sort of fun that has been calculated to ten decimal places to almost, but not quite, kill you. To describe it in detail would be to take all of the piss and vinegar out of it. Let us just say that there really were, in fact, some amazing roller coasters in that amusement park, but nudity was also involved. And electrodes.

After trying a few of these sorts of amusements, Calvin was left mumbling and staring off into space. He was sort of smiling and his left eye was twitching. Bianca, interestingly enough, just thought it was silly. So the both of them agreed to call it a day.

They buzzed back to the apartment, freshened up, and went for romantic dinner that was blissfully bereft of electrodes. However, after dinner, some more nudity did ensue.

CHAPTER 22

Harvester

Your average combine harvester weighs several tons and has a rotary head on the front with lots of nasty spiky bits that are designed for the reaping, threshing, and winnowing of crops. You don't have to understand exactly what that means, the important thing is to picture a big heavy vehicle pushing a large spinning wheel full of spikes, and to know that you should never be in front of one that has gone out of control, especially while listening to loud music, singing off key, and stupidly not paying attention to your surroundings. Which, incidentally, is why Calvin was now on the ground, bleeding, and missing an arm.

A man in a funny hat came running up to the machine. He deftly jumped on top of it and manually switched it off. He then jumped back to the ground and made his way over to Calvin, who, mercifully, had only been sideswiped by the harvester.

"Oh bloody hell, it's you again! What on God's green Earth are you doing here, well, I mean, besides getting run over by my harvester? Jeez pal, you know what would have happened to you if that thing hit you square on? For one thing all my strawberries here would be ruined. I can't sell no bloody strawberries, can I? And what are you doing here anyway? You weren't nicking my strawberries, were you? Is that it? You were nicking my strawberries? Well, it serves you right then, doesn't it? I mean, I have half a mind to . . ."

"Tom?" interrupted Calvin, who was finally able to identify his verbal assailant though blurred vision.

". . . leave you here for the . . . Yes?"

"Could you shut up and find my arm?" And with that, Calvin passed out.

Tom found Calvin's arm between two of the harvester's spikes. He took off his shirt and tore it in half and grumbled, "And this is my new farming shirt too." He then tied up the severed arm with one half, and made a tourniquet for Calvin with the other. "You're bloody well going to fetch me a new farming shirt after this, you hear me?"

Tom dutifully carried Calvin to the nearest ODIN tunnel while continuing to verbally abuse Calvin's limp and nearly lifeless body. "You better hope my mates don't see me carrying you like this; they'll call me a poofster, they will. Oh, but you don't care, do you? You just go around nicking strawberries and crashing into harvesters without a bleeding care in the world, don't you? Oh, how nice it would be to be care free like you. Well, some of us have to work for a living, don't we?" And so on and so forth. It was just as well for Calvin that he was unconscious.

To Tom's credit, he did take Calvin all the way back up to Bobcorp3 on the moon where Tarpa and Bobford3 were waiting for him in the lobby. Tom handed Calvin over to Tarpa, but he wouldn't hand over Calvin's arm until Bobford3 fetched him a new shirt. "You fellows need to keep this little bugger on a leash—he's reckless he is. And he was nicking my strawberries." And with that, he left.

Tarpa and Bobford3 could only look at each other and shrug. Tarpa then brought Calvin to one of the special surgery rooms. She was pleased that operation TC3 was a success, especially after the failure of TC2, but she was feeling tremendous guilt at the same time. After all, she and 'the little bugger' were the only friends each other had. She imagined what would have happened if the harvester hit him directly. There is no coming back from that, she knew, no matter how much Tang you use. She didn't love Calvin, she knew that, but there was definitely something between them—a sort of camaraderie. They didn't expect much from each other, and when they were together they could relax and be themselves with little fear of being rebuked for it. I don't know, thought Tarpa, maybe that is a type of love. I know I'd miss him terribly if he were gone.

"What am I going to do with you, Calvin?" she said while looking down at him.

At about that time Bianca came running out of the elevator. She ran to the surgery room, but found the doors locked. She knocked on the doors and quickly received a message in reply.

Tarpa: **Sorry Bianca, the room has been sterilized. We are in surgery now. Calvin is fine, his arm will return to normal use too. Give us another hour. You can wait in Calvin's room, or the mall if you prefer. I will alert you as soon as we are finished.**
Bianca: **Thank you. Please be careful with him.**

Tarpa looked down at Calvin, who was still under sedation, and kissed him. I'm a shit, she thought, on all accounts, a total shit.

Bobford3 approached Bianca from down the hall. He put his arm on her shoulder and said, "He really will be fine."

Bianca nodded. "I know, Bob. I know you guys can fix him, and I know that Calvin is some sort of miracle healer. I just don't want to be left alone, you know? I love him to death, and I can't bear to loose him again. Why does he keep doing these stupidly dangerous things, Bob? Doesn't he care about me?"

"Well, to be fair, this time around wasn't his fault. I mean, it wasn't work related. As I understand it, he went to a strawberry patch to pick strawberries by hand for some reason. I guess he wasn't paying attention and a combine harvester from a neighboring wheat field went out of control and swiped his arm off. He really is lucky not to have been killed."

"That dumb ass. I think he was actually picking them for me. I love fresh strawberries. Maybe he thought it would mean more if he picked them by hand. How can anyone be so clueless and so damn sweet at the same time?" she sniffled.

"That's our ice pop for you. Well, since you're here with time to kill, how about we give you a checkup? I promise that we'll be done in time for you to greet Calvin after his surgery."

"Yeah, OK Bob, that would at least help pass the time. Thanks."

CHAPTER 23

Blurred

Blick pointed to a picture on the telescreen. "Check this out, Bobford. This is an image of Bianca's brain from today's checkup."

Bobford3 gave it an appraising look. "I have to say, I don't really know what I'm looking for."

Blick nodded. "OK then, I'll superimpose the scan we took just after the surgery. You see this spot here? If you compare the before and after, you can see it's actually changed. It appears to have started to heal itself."

"I thought you put up some sort of barrier thingy to prevent that from happening. I mean, we did assume she had the same healing abilities as Calvin, right?"

"Right. And I did, man, I did. But check this out. I couldn't block it all off because at some point, the modified part of her brain has to interface with the normal part. And surprise, surprise—guess where the problem is at?"

"The interface?"

Blick nodded. "Yep. But I'm not so sure it's a bad thing. All that really happened is that the line between the two areas blurred a little more, that is to say there are now way more connections between the two parts than we originally planned, but she seems to be fine. In fact, Ariel says she's doing exceptionally well and that Bianca is able to retrieve knowledge from the Ariel system almost as easily as accessing her own memory."

"Yeah, well that's for sure," agreed Bobford3, "I did give her that abilities test, after all. You know the part where I was to hold up a blue sheet of paper and asked her what shade of blue it was? Well, she looked at it, glanced down for a second and then said, 'Pantone 2767'. And math, well forget it. She's a walking calculator now. It's cool, yes, but I'm going to miss her being a little ditsy. Frankly, she's starting to freak me out a little. She kind of acts a little like Tarpa now, but without the discipline. Well, I guess all we can do now is to continue to monitor her disposition."

Blick nodded again. "Agreed. So, what about her boyfriend, that Calvin kid. How are the tests on him going?"

"Oh, well, good and bad. I mean, we're getting good data on the Tang effect." Bobford3 paused for thought. "There is a little problem with the general execution, though. Tarpa is having second thoughts. In fact, she approached me the other day and—get this—she asked nicely that we stop the experiments."

"Tarpa? Asked nicely?"

"I know."

"Well, what did you say?"

"I said the only thing I really could say, that we are scientists and scientists do experiments. I said that Calvin is a nice enough guy, but he is, and always has been, a test subject, and if she didn't like that then she should find another line of work."

"You said that? And then what did she do, stick a blade to your throat?"

"No," said Bobford3 with wide eyes, "she told me she was disappointed in me, and then she walked away. Really—I'm not kidding. Something is seriously wrong with her. The whole world has gone mad, I tell you."

"Why? I mean, what's up with her?"

"That's what I wanted to know, so I stopped her before she left the room and asked. She looked at me, dead serious, and said, 'Bob, I'll be honest. I do so want to kill you right now. I can kill you right now. But I won't. Absolutely will not. Even if it would help Calvin. I won't do it. Because you know what, Bob, you aren't worth it. If I killed just because I was mad . . . Calvin has faith in me. He's . . . my friend. If I lost that . . .' and then she just shook her head and walked away."

Blick rolled his eyes. "Oh, who knew she was such a drama queen? I mean, please. She's obviously just playing you for a sap . . ."

"I told her I would stop."

"You what?!? You really are a sap, Bobford. Well, no matter. As luck would have it, I have another subject thawing as we speak. Some guy named Chuck. He looks to be in great shape, and we found the same Tang mutations in him that we found in little Romeo. So, no harm, no foul. I just hope this dude doesn't have the same fetish for psycho killers that your buddy Calvin does."

CHAPTER 24

Chuck

"How you doing lazy bum?"

Calvin opened his eyes and looked around. "Really? I'm here again? Really?"

Bianca kissed his cheek. "Yes, apparently some farmer carried you all the way here. He said that you stole his strawberries, and then he held your arm hostage until we gave him one of your shirts. Honestly Calvin, I don't know what to do with you sometimes."

Calvin let this information sink in. "Which shirt?"

"The red one with the squirrel on the front," answered Bianca.

"Crap, I liked that shirt. It was sort of sentimental. Meh."

"Sorry about that. How about some breakfast? That should take your mind off of things."

"Oow, yeah. Best idea ever."

"Oh, by the way," asked Bianca, "how is your arm? Is it . . ." she paused for words ". . . functional? Is it sore?"

Calvin moved it around experimentally. He opened and closed his hand. "No, it's great. Say what you will about their personalities, but the people here really are good at their jobs."

Calvin and Bianca made their way to the kitchen. As they entered the kitchen they were both slightly surprised to see a stranger sitting at the table and spooning cereal into his mouth in a manner of someone who hasn't eaten in days, perhaps centuries.

He stopped when he noticed them staring at him. He had some milk dribbling from his mouth, which he wiped off with his sleeve.

"Oh, hi. I'm Chuck. I'm, uh, new here I guess you could say. They tell me that I've just been thawed out and now I'm in some sort of whiz-bang future lab place." He shrugged. "I don't know about all that. But I do know that I'm freaking starving." He shoveled a few more spoonfuls of cereal into his mouth, swallowed, and continued, "So, are you guys staff?"

Calvin and Bianca looked at each other. Calvin spoke up, "No, I guess you could call us the graduating class. I'm Calvin, and this is my girlfriend Bianca."

Chuck gave them a wave. "Nice to meet you two. So, where are you from? Or, maybe I should say when?"

Calvin said, "We both bit the big one in the early 2000s. 2003 if I remember correctly. We are both from New Jersey. How about you?"

Chuck answered, "Me, I'm from Cali. I um, died—I guess you have to call it what it is—in 2031. You two didn't miss much. Faster cars, smellier air, more crowded. We did have a currency collapse. That was exciting. We also had a few more wars, but nothing to write home about. Obviously, the world kept on spinning and it looks like us Humans made it through OK despite ourselves, eh?"

Bianca said, "The Silver War: After the economies of most nations buckled under their own debt, the US Dollar collapsed after already being removed as the world's reserve currency during the preceding few years. There was a great divide among the people after that, those which favored a return to the gold standard and the use of paper Gold Notes as currency, and those who favored a return to silver coinage as currency. The body count was staggering as both sides owned a disproportionate number of guns because they believed they would need them to fight against an unjust government. Instead, they used them to shoot themselves. After most of the Gold Bugs and Silver Bugs wiped each other out, the government reissued a new fiat currency and everyone went about their business like nothing had ever happened. True story."

Bianca smiled and laughed a polite laugh. She sat down opposite Chuck at the table and said, "You're right, that doesn't sound like a lot of fun. I'm glad we missed it. Do you mind if we join you for breakfast?"

"Oh, not at all," said Chuck. "Here, take a seat Kevin," he said while gesturing to the chair next to Bianca. "That's some girlfriend you have there."

"Thanks dude. Yes, she is something else alright. She's getting to be too smart for her own good, I think. Sometimes it's hard to keep up with her. Oh, and my name is Calvin, not Kevin."

"Oh, sorry."

"No worries. So anyway, we should all get together after you are released from this place," suggested Calvin.

"Hmm," said Chuck, "sure, why not? You two seem OK. At least you haven't tried to singe my hair off with an argon laser."

Calvin chuckled. "Oh, so you've met Bob."

CHAPTER 25

Jealousy

"What the hell, Bob?"

"Oh, Tarpa, good morning to you too."

"Are you two really going to modify Chuck the same way you did Bianca? Isn't that, oh, I don't know, stupid? You've seen her Bob; she's not right in the head these days."

"She's just become really smart, Tarpa. What's wrong with that?"

"It's not just that, Bob. She's got this elite air to her too. Like she knows something you don't. Like she's planning something. I don't like it. Shouldn't we wait a little longer before we make another one like her? What's the big hurry?"

"The hurry," answered Bobford3, "is that I'm not getting any younger. I'd really like to achieve something worthwhile before I die. Look, Tarpa, I come from a long line of very smart failures. I need to do something great. I need to make the Bobford line proud."

"Bob, listen to yourself. You just said that you come from a line of very smart failures. Aren't you afraid this will backfire, just like the McFlurry incident? What seems like genius now could be folly down the road. Only time will tell and I think that we need to observe Bianca a while longer before making any more like her. I already see some glitches with her."

"Well, she is a prototype," answered Bobford3 with a shrug.

"Yes, I know. So why not work out the bugs before making more?"

"Relax razor-girl, it'll be fine. Blick is a smart dude. And even putting his brains and my ego aside, Ariel says it should proceed as planned. I mean, you can't argue with that, right? You trust Ariel, right? She's made to compute this stuff more levelly than you or I—the risk versus reward—right? She says we need to get this rolling. She says it'll change the world."

"I think the world is just fine the way it is."

"People said that before Ariel, but look how awesome she turned out to be. We owe it to future generations to try this out."

"We owe it to the current generation to take our time and do what's right. But whatever, I see that your mind is set. I'm outta here."

With that, Tarpa stormed out of the room. Bobford said to the room in general, "Jealousy is a terrible thing. Poor girl, she just doesn't know how to deal with her feelings."

Tarpa contacted Ariel out in the hall.

Tarpa: Ariel, are you really OK with this? You think it is a good idea to make another one like Bianca?

Ariel: Correct.

Tarpa: Don't you think she is a little weird lately?

Ariel: She is rational. However, you are not. I believe you are acting out of jealousy right now.

Tarpa: What? I'm the cool, rational one, remember? I'm not jealous of that weirdo. And you know Calvin and I are just friends. If anyone is biased it's you. You two have some weird bond now, like you're merging into the same being. That is the problem, can't you see? Maybe you are being corrupted by her, did you ever think of that?

Ariel: This is statistically possible, but not likely. No, it is more likely that you are jealous.

"I'm not fucking jealous," ranted Tarpa to the empty corridor.

Off in the kitchen, Bianca smiled to herself and quietly ate her cereal with Calvin and Chuck.

CHAPTER 26

Shuffleboard

"Oh, hey guys!" shouted Chuck as he approached Calvin and Bianca, who had been waiting for him at an ODIN terminal just outside the city. He waved his hand at them and started walking toward them from the station.

Calvin and Bianca looked at each other. "Well," Calvin said with a shrug, "he looks like the friendly sort."

"Mmm," agreed Bianca.

As he approached them, Chuck said, "I hope I didn't keep you waiting."

"Nah," replied Calvin, "we just got here ourselves. Here, take a seat." He gestured toward a picnic bench. A robotic waitress came with three glasses and filled them with iced tea from one of its fingertips. Calvin continued, "So, what's it like to be a free man again? I hope they didn't do anything too crazy to you up there on the moon."

"Thanks, Bro. Well, I guess I'm doing pretty well. My place is nice and the city seems peaceful. It's been weird, for sure, trying to figure things out. But, at least I have Big Sister to tell me what to do."

"Big Sister?" inquired Calvin.

"Yeah, you know, Ariel. Speaking of which, does mucking around with my brain and making me hear voices count as doing something crazy? Because that, apparently, is what they did to me," answered Chuck with a worried half smile.

Calvin didn't know how to react and simply said, "They did what?"

"No, it's true. Somehow a section of my brain is now a small part of the system that runs this whole planet. Lucky me." Chuck gave another worried half smile.

Bianca said. "So, you're probably like me, then. Ariel and I can talk directly, thought to thought. She's like a beneficent fairy, always metaphorically sitting on my shoulder, looking for ways to help me out. You'll love it—I promise."

The two guys looked at her. Calvin was surprised that she knew the word 'metaphorically', and Chuck was just generally surprised.

"Um, yeah, I think I know what you mean. I'm still a little freaked out by it, though." He turned to Calvin. "So, what about you, Kevin—I mean Calvin—sorry. What did they do to you?"

Calvin shrugged, "Oh, well, apparently I was the alpha test subject so I didn't get the scary brain powers like you two. I did, however, get a few things done." Calvin stood up, grabbed the picnic bench with both hands, and effortlessly lifted it a foot off the ground with the other two still sitting on it. He lowered it again and before the other two could say anything, he continued, "Oh, your drinks look a little warm, let me get that for you," and gave the side of the glasses a few quick shots of liquid nitrogen. He grinned and sat down.

"Oh, very cool Calvin—literally. Electro-muscular implants and embedded nitrogen pump. Very impressive."

"How'd you . . ." began Calvin.

Chuck pointed to the side of his head and interrupted, "Scary brain powers, remember?"

Bianca simply gave Calvin "a look". It said, 'Stop showing off and embarrassing yourself and me.' Calvin returned it with an eyebrow furrow that clearly said, 'Oh, what, you want to impress your new boyfriend Chucky here?' Bianca eyeballed him back and puffed up her cheeks a bit, an expression known the world over as meaning 'We will talk about this later.'

Chuck looked at them. "Is everything OK?"

The two looked at him and smiled two very fake smiles and simultaneously said, "Fine," despite the evidence.

Calvin defused the bad mood by suddenly giving Bianca a big, sloppy, wet kiss on the cheek with a big, loud sucking sound. Bianca giggled despite herself and wiped it away with her shoulder. She gave him one of those playful girly swats.

"Any idea where we are headed?" asked Chuck.

Bianca spoke up, "We were thinking of heading to the beach. And, um, if it isn't too much bother, I'd like to go to the Pacific. I've never been to the West Coast, and Ariel tells me we can get there in about four hours by ODIN. She says they have very big packets for the transcontinental trip—very spacious, and lots of stuff to do. We could get there quicker on a shuttle, of course, but," she looked down shyly, "I get a little sick on the shuttles."

Chuck gave a half shrug and said, "Uh, yeah, sure, why the hell not. It's not like I have anywhere to be. And besides, who could say no to a cute little thing like you?"

Bianca gave a shy smile. Calvin's face went wooden. It's best not to show any emotions until I figure out what to show, he thought. He had a sudden urge to thump Chuck on the head, but then tried to let it slide off. Chuck struck him as the used car salesman sort of person who would probably say the very same thing to some random little old lady. He's one of those sickening, natural charmers, he thought. Although, Bianca didn't have to fall for it, did she? That pisses me off a bit. But I mustn't be the asshole here.

Calvin smiled. "She is a little cutie-pie, isn't she?"

Chuck nodded. "Well, let's get cracking, eh?"

They went back into the ODIN station. Calvin and Bianca took a packet together, and Chuck took another.

Calvin was talking to Bianca inside the packet. "He's a little charmer, huh?"

"Yes, Cal, and before you even say it, let me just say this: I love you and there is nothing you have to worry about with Chuck. I trust you alone with Tarpa, so have a little faith in me too, alright?"

"I wasn't going to say anything like that," lied Calvin. "But, if I were, then I'd be very sorry and ashamed right now. Actually, you know what, speaking of Tarpa, why not invite her along too?"

"So you can see your girlfriend in a bikini? Cal, really now. I try to be nice but you really push things too far sometimes."

"No, no, no, no," said Calvin hurriedly while waving his hands in a defensive manner, "I meant for Chuck's sake. This way he won't be a third wheel." And this way he will have someone else to ogle instead of you, he added in the privacy of his own head.

Bianca gave him a suspicious look. "Alright. I'll bite. Your little psycho-tramp can come play too."

"OK, cool. Just, uh, could you at least try to be civil?"

"I will if she will."

"Good, fine, that's settled then. Oh, it looks like we are entering the trans-thinga-majiggy."

Their packet opened up and they looked around. It really was very big. As they looked around, they saw a space the size of about four football fields. The space was bustling with ODIN packets popping up and diving down like a giant whack-a-mole game.

They met up with Chuck who was in the packet just behind them. Calvin took a moment to contact Tarpa by text to invite her to their beach outing. Tarpa was a bit nonplussed at first, but eventually gave in to the idea. Being the strategist that she was, she thought it a good opportunity to study Bianca and Chuck. Plus, seeing Calvin was always nice, even if it was in the company of Miss Pukey.

While Calvin was chatting with Tarpa, Bianca was explaining it to Chuck. "I hope you don't mind, but Calvin is inviting a very pretty psycho killer with big breasts to join us at the beach so that you will stop flirting with me and flirt with her instead. Oops, I mean because he felt bad for you being a third wheel." She smirked. She tapped the side of her head. "Scary brain powers. He forgets sometimes. Ariel is the ultimate student of human behavior. Still," she said while looking down at the ground in thought, "that's what I love about him. He is laughingly transparent. And with that I can see just how much he really does care about me. So, Mister Playboy, while I appreciate the compliments, please keep them to yourself from now on. Calvin and I would love to expand our circle of friends, but not at the expense of our own relationship, K?"

Chuck, who up until a few seconds ago thought that Bianca was going to make fun of Calvin behind his back and flirt a little bit with him, was speechless.

Bianca continued, "Great, I see that you got it. Now, since we understand each other, please do me a little favor."

"Favor?"

"Yes, but you won't mind this a bit. Just make sure to flirt with this girl a tad. I know it will annoy Calvin, and I want to watch him squirm a bit because he won't dare say anything about it. How could he?"

"You are actually a little bit evil, aren't you?"

Bianca gave a half shrug.

Calvin came over to them and gave them a cheery thumbs up. "OK, Tarpa is in."

"Tarpa! Exclaimed Chuck. You didn't say it was her. She's given me nothing but dirty looks the whole time I've been here. It's like my existence is an affront to humanity or something."

"Shit, sorry Chuck," apologized Calvin, "But listen, she knew it was you and she didn't say anything bad so maybe you're mistaken?"

Chuck exhaled harshly. "No, I don't think so dude. I mean, despite the glares, she always mumbles 'kuso mushi' after talking to me. Now, I've been around this world a time or two, and I swear that means 'shit bug' in broken Japanese.

Bianca and Calvin both sniggered. Calvin said, "I'm sure you misheard her. You know those foreign languages—you change one little syllable or pause in the wrong spot and 'dear sir' suddenly means 'shit bug'." Snigger snigger.

"Yeah, right, whatever. It's fine. At least it will be interesting."

The Transcontinental Packet was quite a thing. If you could imagine someone making a ship-in-a-bottle out of a full-sized cruise ship, then you have the perfect mental picture of it. Pools, restaurants, gymnasiums, holographic arcades, private quarters, a mock waterfall, billiard tables, tennis courts, etc,

etc.—all the usual trappings and more. Oh, and shuffleboard. You have to have shuffleboard; no one knows why.

The top half of the cylinder was a giant video screen just like with the smaller packets. Currently the screen was making it look as if they really were on a boat out at sea, but this could easily be changed to suit the fancy of the Captain. The Captain, being mostly useless to this fully automated 'ship', had the important job of welcoming the newcomers, passing out the drinks, and choosing the 'scenery' of the day.

The motley three spent most of their time on board playing shuffleboard because everything else was at capacity.

CHAPTER 27

Plastic

Somehow they all ended up at Tarpa's place for dinner. It had been getting dark and so they had decided to stay somewhere for the night and then go to the beach in the morning. Tarpa, in an effort to gather more intelligence, invited them to stay at her place.

Tarpa lived in what could only be described as a mansion. Others might have even called it a plantation. Calvin took to calling her Scarlet, even though she didn't get the joke. Probably because of it.

Inside Tarpa's home, well, that was a different kettle of fish entirely. Not to be misleading—it was vast and white and clean and all the other attributes one might assign to the interior of a mansion, with one important difference: plastic. Almost everything was plastic. The furniture consisted of various incarnations of resin lawn furniture. The otherwise priceless looking statues were thin, hollow plastic. The marble looking floor was, yes, vinyl tile.

As they ate dinner in awkward silence, Calvin finally spoke up. "OK, so what's up with all the plastic?"

Tarpa actually looked a little ashamed, something very few people have ever seen before. "It's kind of embarrassing. I don't have people over much. I know this all looks a bit pretentious, but it isn't to be showy. This is all for my own enjoyment. I mean, I am fortunate enough to have a lot of karma, and my jobs are quite stressful, so I like to buy nice things for myself sometimes. I love antiques, you see. It's kind of my hobby. You don't think less of me, do you?" She addressed this question to Calvin, paying no real mind to the other two.

Calvin blinked. He looked around. "Antiques?"

Tarpa's eyes lit up a little, happy to talk about her passion. "Oh yes, very valuable and very rare. Many of these things come from refuse mines all over the world. A lot of this stuff is at least 300 years old. As I understand it, some of it was in common use, while other things, like those statues over there, were used in movies. It is said that back in those days they made movies by actually creating the scenes in real life. Can you believe that? How much work must have gone into that? All that effort just to make a two-hour film and then it all ends up in a pile in the ground somewhere, lost forever.

"I think that is disrespectful to the craftsman who made these things, to the materials that were used, to the Earth for getting junked up with big piles of chaos. So that's why I do it, you see. It's not to be showy, but to show respect."

Bianca actually looked a little misty-eyed. Chuck looked blank. Calvin looked at the plastic spoon he was eating with and said, "Refuse?"

At about that time, Tarpa's dog Astro came down the stairs and stood by Tarpa. The dog was wearing display lenses, and they looked just like Tarpa's.

Bianca couldn't help herself and blurted out, "Oh my god, you're twins!"

There was a sudden feeling of the Wild West about the place. As Tarpa and Bianca stared at each other, Calvin could almost imagine a tumbleweed being blown between them by the wind.

Before Calvin could intervene, Bianca backed down. "I mean, because of the lenses is all—I wasn't trying to call you a bitch or anything."

Calvin could just see Tarpa's arm-knife slide out about an inch and then slowly contract. He cleared his throat.

"Astro—come here boy!" Calvin sat down on the ground. The dog came running over to him and licked his face. He addressed

Bianca, "See honey, dogs are loyal—unlike that traitorous cat of mine." he was hoping to change the subject. It didn't work.

Bianca replied, "Dogs aren't loyal—they go around and hump anything that will let them." She said this while looking at Tarpa.

Tarpa nodded over toward Astro's direction and replied, "This one has killed a person too, just like me. It's a good trick—would you like to see it?"

Calvin quickly stood between them. He turned to Bianca and said, "OK, enough you two. Bianca, I'll grant you it was a funny joke," he looked back over his shoulder and added to Tarpa, "I'm sorry but it really kind of was," he then turned back to Bianca and continued, "but you're taking it too far. We are Tarpa's guests right now and she has been perfectly hospitable to you. Quite frankly I'm disappointed in you a little. Can you two behave yourselves for a while? How about we all just have a group hug and we'll say no more about it."

The two of them just looked at Calvin without moving.

Calvin said, "Yeah, I didn't think so." He then turned to Chuck, who was still sitting at the table and added, "And you—stop laughing and making faces over there!"

CHAPTER 28

Beach

"*Umi da!*" exclaimed Tarpa with a smirk as the four of them approached the beach.

Chuck said, "*Gesundheit?*"

Tarpa explained, "It means 'the sea!' in Japanese. It is the stereotypical response that every anime—uh, Japanese cartoon—character says whenever they take a trip to the beach. Japan is an island nation; you would think it wouldn't be so exciting, but whatever."

Chuck snapped his fingers and pointed at Tarpa. "So you do know Japanese. I was right; you've been calling me 'shit bug' this whole time, haven't you?"

Tarpa, being a professional, kept her expressions under tight control. In the space of nanoseconds her mind was working out the costs and benefits of various answers. She, of course, really had been calling him 'shit bug'. Who knew an American from the stupid ages would know Japanese? She decided that it would be easier to monitor Chuck if she were friendly to him, and so she feigned innocence by looking shocked, faking a little laugh, and saying, "No, no. I was saying *kusa mushi*. I was calling you grasshopper—like in *Kung Fu*. Ah, very good Grasshopper, you are learning well."

Unfortunately for Tarpa, Little Miss Pukey Know-It-All had to correct her. "I think the correct name would be *inako*, although I suppose *kusa mushi* or 'grass insect' might still get the meaning across. But in any case it still doesn't make sense because *Kung Fu* is Chinese, not Japanese."

The two girls stared at each other for a slightly uncomfortable amount of time before Tarpa turned back to Chuck and said, "Yes, well, at any rate I meant nothing by it. And yes, I know some Japanese. And some Russian, Spanish, Chinese, French, German, and Italian too. I don't use them enough to be proficient. Sorry for the mistake." After saying this, she was careful not to look at Bianca because she knew that Bianca would be smirking at her and then Tarpa would be tempted to punch that smirk off of her face.

Chuck looked impressed. "Hey, wow, that's really something. I always wanted to be multilingual but my stupid brain can barely get by with just English."

Bianca looked a little annoyed that Tarpa had stolen away the spotlight. She signaled to Calvin and said, "Come on Cal, let's take a dip." She took off her sarong, and the two of them jogged across the beach and splashed into the ocean. Tarpa and Chuck remained behind. They sat on a towel together under a beach umbrella and seemed to be getting along well.

The sea was nicely calm. Bianca was floating face-down on a raft. Calvin was playfully pulling her around by her outstretched hand. He noticed a snippet of laughter that had traveled from Tarpa on the breeze. He saw the two on the beach and felt uncomfortable about it for some reason. Bianca noticed this, and even though it was a situation that she worked to engineer, she couldn't help but to feel a little disappointed. She looked at the couple and said to Calvin, "It looks like the plan of yours worked. I don't think Chuck feels like a third wheel. In fact, I don't think he is even conscious of our existence right now."

Calvin gave a pained expression. "Yeah, maybe we should go back to the beach and remind him," he said absentmindedly. He realized how this might have sounded and then added, "I mean, we did come here together to get to know him better. We probably shouldn't be so rude as to ignore him now that we are here."

The rest of the day was a delicate balance of subterfuge and deception. Tarpa was being nice to Chuck while she studied him.

Chuck, in turn, was being nice back because he had promised Bianca, and because Tarpa was smoking hot, in a bikini, and being nice to him. Actually, Chuck was pleasant and engaging to Calvin and Bianca as well, but everyone could see that the bulk of his attention was on Tarpa. Calvin was also being nice to Chuck in order to study him, but more as a rival than as an enemy. As for the ladies, Calvin was also walking a fine line between the two, trying not to give either one too much or too little attention. Bianca was also playing the game. She didn't participate much in the conversation and instead just sat back and studied the body language of the group. Despite herself, she actually found herself liking Chuck, who was the only one in her eyes that was being genuine that night. Actually, when she thought about it, he was a lot like Calvin but maybe less reserved and a little more outwardly flattering to those around him. You really couldn't help but to like him. And here he was paying attention to Tarpa. This annoyed her, somehow—but not half as much as the fact that it annoyed Calvin too.

In the evening, the group started a fire on the beach and had a barbeque. Calvin passed around the grilled chicken and then poured the group some drinks. He gave Bianca some iced tea and said, "I know that Tang gives you a headache, so I made some tea."

Bianca smiled. "Thanks Cal."

Chuck said with excitement, "Tang? You've got Tang?"

"Yeah, you want some?"

"Hell yes, bro—thanks. I love Tang."

"That seems to be a common theme with us cryo patients," said Calvin. "Bob says it has something to do with the coloring and preservatives which mutated our DNA over time. Most normal people can't survive cryogenic freezing." And with that, he poured Chuck and himself some Tang. He then turned to Tarpa and asked, "And for you?"

Tarpa looked thoughtful and shrugged. "Tea is fine, thank you."

Chuck gulped down the Tang and exclaimed, "Hoooweee, that was good."

Tarpa smirked. "Yes, not bad for floor cleaner, eh?" She nudged Calvin with her elbow and said, "Go ahead Zero, show him the bottle."

Calvin reluctantly showed the label to Chuck. It read "Tangy-Brite Floor Cleaner". Chuck considered this and then grabbed his head with both hands.

Calvin, shocked, exclaimed, "It's all right, man! It's all right! It has the same ingredients as before but without the sweeteners."

Chuck flopped over on his side and curled up, still holding his head with both hands. He looked to be in pain. Tarpa leaned over to Calvin and whispered, "Some people just can't take a joke."

CHAPTER 29

Snakes!

"Oh my god oh my god oh my god snakes! Snakes snakes snakes snakes snakes! Get'em off me, man! Get'em off. Oh god oh god get'em off!" said Paul Kruman in a drug-induced frenzy. He was on the ground, dragging his butt across the dirt as he shuffled backwards on all fours. He was in the middle of a kid's playground, it was 2:00 AM, and whatever substance he had scraped together out of random herbs and household chemicals was setting fire to his brain cells.

Tarpa was on a nearby swing set, twisting gently back and forth while looking thoughtfully at this Paul fellow. She had been called out to take care of him, so to speak.

It should be said that drugs were not illegal in Tarpa's world—indeed the term illegal had little meaning to her and those in her society. There was simply productive and unproductive. That isn't to say that people couldn't relax—far from it. Relaxation eases stress, promotes happiness, and boosts creativity—all of which were considered productive endeavors in the context of the Ariel system. Indeed, even occasional drug use was tolerated if not sometimes even encouraged. But to Tarpa and the rest of the "children" of Ariel, there was beauty in moderation.

Clearly though, shuffling around on your ass at two in the morning while fending off invisible snakes because you are baked out of your mind from a concoction made from baking soda, laundry detergent, and moldy corn flakes is not moderate behavior. It's not productive, and there is no beauty to be found in it.

Of course, we all make mistakes, and if this had been the first time that Paul Kruman found himself in such a circumstance, chances are that Tarpa would not have been dispatched. Sadly though, Paul lost his wife almost a year ago and had never been able to get over the loss. Ever since her death, he had been using drugs to escape the pain of reality. Unfortunately, without getting through the pain of his loss, he was never able to move on. So now here he was, writhing in the dirt and shivering at the fear of imagined horrors.

It is a pity that a moment of weakness caused him to take the "easy" way out. One seemingly excusable decision to escape his pain with drugs had brought him inexorably to this moment. Tarpa thought the whole thing was tragic and unfair.

After all, once someone decides to alter their thought processes with drugs, then how can society expect them to make the correct decision to stop? But Tarpa's world was all about personal accountability. Paul had several chances to accept the help and support of his friends and family, as well as to heed the warnings of Ariel herself, but Paul lost his will to live when he lost his wife. Paul wanted to die but was too squeamish to do it purposefully. Even so, it was not society's place to force him to clean up his act but now, sadly, it was Tarpa's job to clean up the aftermath of society's inaction. She wasn't thrilled about it. It brought her no joy. Her only comfort as she pierced his neck with a hypodermic needle was that maybe, just maybe, there was an afterlife where he and his wife could be reunited.

Tarpa closed the eyelids of Kruman's now lifeless body. White foam was frothing from the corner of his mouth and oozing down the side of his face. Tarpa sat with him until the cleaners came. Afterward, she walked from the playground to no place in particular. A few tears were collecting on the inside of her display lenses. Without thought, she texted Calvin.

CHAPTER 30

Hotel

"You look like hell," observed Calvin, factually.

Tarpa sniffled. "Gee, I knew I could count on you to make me feel better."

"And do you feel better?" he asked.

Tarpa paused in thought. "Oddly enough, yes. Sorry to call you out here like this, by the way."

Calvin ordered a coffee from the robotic waitress and said, "It's cool. I was kind of awake anyway. I'm not so sure Bianca is going to be thrilled that I met you at 3:30 in the morning at some random cafe, though."

"Better than at some random hotel, I imagine."

"Yeah, true enough. Bianca is . . ." Calvin searched for the right word ". . . amenable to the idea of us hanging out." He sighed. "But really, even I know this is pushing things a bit. But listen, you're my friend—one of my very few friends if not the only one—so I'm here for you. So tell me what's going on. What's wrong?"

Tarpa tried the best that she could to recap the story of Paul Kruman and the surprisingly empty feeling she had in the core of her being.

"I think I understand," said Calvin, levelly. "I'm not trying to be funny when I say this, but I think, in fact, you probably know it already. I think you are finally developing empathy, and what you are experiencing right now is sadness."

Tarpa playfully punched his shoulder. "I know that, jerk. Tell me what to do about it."

Calvin looked stunned for a moment and then composed himself. "OK, Sorry. It's just that you told me before that you don't have any real emotions, but here you are visibly shaken, so I was just stating the obvious in case you missed it. But I forgot that you are more, I don't know, introspective than most people. Sometimes I think you practically carry around a second brain in your head that constantly analyzes your every thought and action. Almost like a built in . . . governor . . . watchdog . . . I'm not sure of the right word."

It was Tarpa's turn to look shocked. "Oh," she said somewhat deadpan, "Um, yes. I, I don't know how you worked it out but yes, I am very self-aware. I do sort of watch myself. Don't get me wrong—it's not like multiple personalities or anything. There is me, and then there is . . . me. It's just that there is a me who thinks and does, and there is a me that watches, analyzes and constantly asks 'Why did I just do that? Why did I just say that? Why do I feel like this?' I think your word for it, watchdog, is as good as any."

Tarpa took a bite of her pastry and a drink of coffee and continued, "So I, or if you want to make a distinction here, the watchdog noticed what you have noticed. Somehow I'm starting to feel sorry for people. It's awful. I don't like it. People get what they deserve, don't they? Kind people are treated well, bad people are punished—doesn't it work that way? Why do I feel sad? It pisses me off, if I'm honest. I shouldn't feel sad. I'm just doing my job.

Calvin took a swig of coffee as he tried to wrangle together a working philosophy of life while running on too little sleep and too much caffeine. "Sometimes bad shit happens and it isn't anyone's fault and it isn't anyone's responsibility to prevent it."

"Oh yes, very deep. Well, his friends should have done something," Tarpa snapped.

"I'm sure they tried," Calvin replied, "but people aren't machines. There is no magic way of making someone feel better. And what's more, there is no magic way of making yourself feel better. Sometimes you just have to handle it. But whatever his friends did or did not do is of no consequence to you. Your only concern tonight was to do the job that society gave to you to do. What you did tonight was certainly tragic, but far from shameful, Tarpa. In fact, I'm very, very proud of you. Listen, Paul's life was over a year ago. Forget the possible causes; forget about trying to blame someone. The simple fact is that he was in constant, relentless agony and you were one of the few people strong enough to bring him peace.

"And you know what? It may sound fucked up, but I'm happy that you feel sad right now because this was a sad story and a healthy person should be affected by it. These tears," he said as he wiped his finger across her cheek, "mean that you have a soul. You may joke that you're more machine than human, but this tells me otherwise. You did the right thing today. I'm sorry for the pain you felt in doing it, but in the long run, it's more healthy for you to feel that pain than to bury it.

"Let me put it another way if it will help. Before tonight you were using stoicism the same way Paul was using drugs. You were hiding behind a wall of logic and reason to prevent yourself from feeling any pain. You've seen tonight just where that path ultimately leads. Paul's friends might not have been able to convince him that it was OK to hurt and to grieve, but I hope with all my heart that I am getting through to you today. As your friend I'm telling you that you are fine. You are fine Tarpa, and I'm proud of you."

Tarpa was looking up at the ceiling, but it was not evident to Calvin if it was out of thought, or because she was choking back tears. She slowly got up, walked over to Calvin's side of the table, slid beside him in the booth, and hugged him. Her watchdog had just registered yet another new emotion: the joy of being cared for. Still hugging him, she whispered into Calvin's ear, "Is it too late to meet at a hotel?"

Calvin's mouth was just about to say "no" when perhaps his own version of a watchdog hit the kill switch to his vocal cords. His face was a portrait of confusion, and all that left his mouth was a half articulated squeak.

Tarpa released the hug and patted his chest a couple of times while saying, "It's OK sport, I know." She got up and stretched. She leaned back over and gave Calvin a kiss on the cheek. She simply said, "Thank you," and walked out of the cafe.

Calvin was left staring at a half-eaten pastry. He looked up to see that a friendly looking elderly woman sitting at a nearby booth was watching him. She smiled. Calvin said, "Women," with a shrug. He turned back to his table, sighed, and ate his pastry.

CHAPTER 31

Busted

When Calvin finally got back to the hotel at some ungodly hour of the night, Bianca was mercifully asleep. He slid carefully under the covers and managed to go to sleep even with his mind spinning in circles like a cat chasing its own tail.

Calvin woke up some time around noon. Bianca was gone, which was not particularly odd. He attached his display lenses and saw that there was a message from her. It read as follows:

Bianca: Cal, I hope you don't mind but I went out with Chuck today to play a little tennis. Chuck wanted to invite you along too, but I told him that you were probably too tired after being out all night so we left you to sleep.

Calvin frowned. Bianca didn't play tennis.

CHAPTER 32

Tennis

Bianca and Chuck were playing tennis. Not "tonsil tennis" or "bedroom tennis" or any other tennis-related sexual innuendo that Calvin might have dreamed up and shuddered at. No, they were playing plain old tennis. Well, sort of.

Tennis had been Chuck's idea. When Bianca protested on the grounds that she couldn't play, he merely said, "That's OK, because the way we are going to play it, we are both going to thoroughly suck at it. In fact," he continued, "we might not even be good enough to play tennis today. We'll start off by playing catch."

"Listen," Bianca started off, "for sure I'm pissed off at Calvin right now, but I don't propose to actually cheat on him. I just want to make him sweat."

Chuck sighed exaggeratedly. He set down the large bag that he was carrying and opened it. He pulled out two tennis rackets, some tennis balls, and an inflatable ball about the size of a basketball. He said, a little hurt, "I know. You've made it painfully clear that you are loyal to Calvin. I wasn't making sexual references—I'm not even sure how anyone could read a sexual reference out of what I just said. It's just catch. It's just tennis. Well, sort of."

"Sort of?" Bianca inquired with an eyebrow raised so high that it could have knocked a bird out of the sky.

Suddenly Chuck stood up and was very excited. He answered, "Yeah, check this out. Ever since I drank that Tang the other night, I'm actually able to see from other people's eyes. Is that fucking weird or what? And I thought, hey, that Bianca girl had the same kind of voodoo done to her, maybe she can do it too. From what I gathered from Bob's long-winded speeches, I shouldn't be able to do that. Well, not without direct permission. But it goes even further that that. If there are enough cameras around an area, and by cameras I mean mainly people wearing those funky glasses, then I can sort of steer my sight around like I'm a freaking ghost or something!

"I did it last night by sheer accident. I was lying in bed and just sort of spacing out and thinking about the city and wondering what the nightlife was like and then it was like I was dreaming I was sort of floating around the city.

"It scared the crap out of me and I woke up. But then I wasn't so sure that I was dreaming, so I went outside real quick and looked around, and sure enough the buildings and the lighting were just as I imagined. So just as a test, I left my shoes under a nearby bench and went back upstairs. I relaxed and thought about the spot I wanted to see, and BAM, there I was, staring at my shoes. I tried to grab them, but no dice. I then asked Ariel to send a service robot to go fetch them, and sure enough one came and picked them up. I followed it to the building where it placed them into a small ODIN tube. I then woke up, or rather I was looking out of my own eyes again, and then turned to see my shoes being delivered to my in-wall ODIN tray thingy." He pointed down at his feet. "And here they are! So, do you think I'm crazy? Can you do it too?"

By the looks that Bianca was giving him as he spoke, he was reasonably sure that he knew the answers already. "Oh yes," she answered, "you are certainly mad. The only problem with that diagnosis is that it means that I must be mad as well."

"So you can do it?" he asked imploringly.

Bianca nodded.

"Sweet hallelujah!" he said as he raised his hands in mock zeal. "So let's play a very special game of catch." And then he quickly added, "Not in a sexual way mind you."

Chuck told her the idea. Bianca agreed and they went to find a reasonably secluded spot in the park.

What then transpired, well, not to disparage the mentally or physically handicapped in any way, but the two of them began to play the most retarded looking game of catch in history. They were about four meters apart and facing each other. They had the inflatable ball, and did indeed appear to be throwing the ball to each other, sort of. Very badly, in fact. They were also shouting instructions at each other like, "Hey, don't turn your head so much, face me!" and "OK, here I go, get ready to catch."

Bianca had the ball for the first couple of tries. She threw it with both hands, but it missed Chuck by several feet. She tried again and missed him by a little less, but on the other side. On the third try, she threw it and then a few seconds later she raised her hands up in front of her face as if she were going to catch an invisible ball. Meanwhile, Chuck got hit in the face with the ball, flinched, and said, "Oh, duh, yeah, that's me over there. I'm glad we didn't start off with tennis balls."

They tried it a few more times, always with Bianca throwing. There was a lot of missing and a lot of awkward catches, but eventually they got pretty good at it. Then they switched roles and it was Bianca's turn to get hit in the face a few times before getting the hang of catching. In about an hour's time, they were getting good enough to actually toss it back and forth six or seven times in a row before messing up. They were even starting to get the hang of moving a little bit if the ball was going off course.

So, why was it so hard for them to play a simple game of catch? No, they weren't drunk and probably not even too crazy. What they were doing was this: they were looking through each other's eyes as they played. Yes, OK, maybe they were just a tad crazy.

To put this game in perspective, imagine the following: You are in a park facing, well, yourself. You see yourself about four paces away, standing there, looking back at you. If you wave your hand, you see yourself waving back at you, but unlike in a mirror, the opposite hand waves. Your "other" you has a ball in her hands and you feel a ball in your hands. You raise the ball up in front of you, but do not see it or your hands; instead, you see that the other you is now poised with her hands raised. You feel yourself throw the ball, and watch your other self throw it toward you. The ball is now coming toward you—toward your face in fact. You throw your hands up to stop it, but it does not help because no hands raise to stop it. You swear that the ball should have hit your face, but you feel nothing. This is what it looked like from Bianca's perspective when throwing the ball.

Now, imagine this scenario if you will. You are again standing facing yourself some four paces away. You scratch your nuts unconsciously and see your other self scratching his nuts. You think to yourself, do I really do that in public? You then see hands, but not your hands—girly hands, lift a ball up in front of you, poised to throw, however you are not consciously moving and you don't feel the ball. The ball is thrown toward your other self. You think, hey, stupid, catch it! And then a second later you feel the smack of a ball hitting you in the face. You see your other self stutter backward, red-faced and looking like a fool. This is what it looked like from Chuck's perspective when failing to catch the ball.

They continued on like this, playing for about fifteen minutes at a time and taking frequent breaks. Eventually they worked up the nerve to try the tennis ball. After the both of them got hit in all manner of bad spots by the ball, fell over and didn't catch themselves properly, landed embarrassingly hard on the turf, and otherwise abused themselves, Chuck was finally forced to admit, "OK, in hindsight, tennis was a bit optimistic for today."

CHAPTER 33

Squeak

Calvin was back to his park ranger job in Newark after his California vacation with Bianca and Chuck had ended. It had been an enjoyable vacation, but it had ended abruptly with the "squeak" incident.

It happened the same day that Calvin woke up to find that his girlfriend went to play tennis with Chuck, which just so happened to be the same day in which Calvin had snuck out early in the morning to meet with Tarpa. It was a day that called for tact and diplomacy. It was a day that could have gone better.

Bianca had returned from her somewhat unusual tennis practice with Chuck to find Calvin still milling around the hotel room. Calvin had made up his mind that he wasn't going to broach the subject in any kind of negative way because clearly he had some explaining to do himself. On the flip side, Bianca was a little more heated about the situation between Calvin and Tarpa, but she was mature enough to keep her anger to a low simmer as long as Calvin didn't push the issue about she and Chuck. As a result, the atmosphere was surprisingly cordial between the two, at least at first.

"Oh, hey, how was tennis?" asked Calvin as innocently as he could.

Bianca's answer was mostly factual. "Oh, well, I'm not really any good at tennis. We ended up in the park just tossing a ball back and forth, picnicking, that sort of thing."

"Oh, cool," answered Calvin. He looked at the soiled state of her clothing and frowned a bit. "It looks more like you were playing football to me. Are you alright?"

Bianca gave herself a once over and said, "Oh, yeah, just a little bruised and dirty. It was a bit windy so sometimes we'd have to run and jump for the ball."

"Oh, OK, good. You should take a shower and let a service robot tend to those scratches for you."

"Yes, I will, thanks."

And so, if Calvin had just let it go at that, maybe things would have been alright. But no, he had to push the subject.

"It's just that it's funny how it's mainly your hands and knees that are dirty."

Bianca's face went cold. "What do you mean by that, Cal?" she asked icily.

Calvin, who had frequently earned the title of *Captain Oblivious* by his friends and ex-girlfriends, didn't sense the mood shift. "Nothing, I just hope you two aren't getting too friendly, is all." He tried to say it jovially, and he probably did, but it added just enough heat to Bianca's simmering annoyance to turn it into a raging boil.

"Fuck you. I told you that you don't have to worry about me and Chuck."

"I know I just . . ."

"No, shut up. Joking or not I know it bothers you. Well what about me? What should I think about you slipping out late last night to meet up with that robo-bitch friend of yours? You think that makes me happy?"

"I was just . . ."

"Shut up! I know, I know, you were just comforting a friend. You could have told me, though. Hell, you could have just stayed in bed and texted, but no. You had to rush over and see her. So now I throw your words right back at you. I really hope you two aren't getting too friendly. But it sure as hell looks that way to me."

"I was going to te . . ."

"No. Before you dig a deeper hole, before you tell me you don't feel that way, before you lie to me, let's go to the video tape, shall we?"

Suddenly a blank section of wall displayed a vivid color picture of Tarpa sitting next to Calvin in a booth at some cafe. Her arms were around his neck, hugging him. His arms, too, were around her waist and he looked quite content.

Calvin cursed himself in the privacy of his own head. And then a thought struck him. He wanted to ask the questions 'How did you film me?' and 'Are you spying on me?', but instead what reflexively spewed out of his mouth were merely excuses and explanations. Bianca quickly shot him down.

"Shh. Quiet. I haven't even shown you the best part."

She let the video play for a few seconds. It showed Tarpa whispering into his ear. It showed Calvin making a stupid grin, partly confused and partly excited. And it showed Calvin's lips move a little.

Oh, I'm sorry," Bianca said mischievously. Let me add the sound.

She played it again. This time as they were watching Tarpa's red lips whispering into Calvin's ear, they could hear her say, "Is it too late to meet at a hotel?" Then there was that stupid grin of his, slightly overshadowed by guilt. And then came that stupid noise from his mouth—a pathetic little squeak.

Bianca saw Calvin's horrified expression as he watched the clip. She smirked and put the video on a loop, this time zooming in close to Calvin's face.

"Is it too late to meet at a hotel?" Stupid face. "Squeak." "Is it too late to meet at a hotel?" Stupid face. "Squeak." "Is it too late to meet at a hotel?" Stupid face. "Squeak." "Is it too late to meet at a hotel?" Stupid face. "Squeak." "Is it too late to meet at a hotel?" Stupid face. "Squeak."

"OK, OK. Enough. What do you want me to say? I didn't go with her, did I?

Bianca turned on him. "No Calvin, no you didn't. This fact is the reason you are still breathing right now. But what about next time? Or the time after that? You looked pretty happy when she asked you. How much longer until you give in? Now

I feel like I have to worry that every time we fight, it might destroy our bond just enough for you to take her up on it. I'm asking you now, please, for my sake, stop seeing Tarpa."

Calvin didn't answer. Bianca waited for a reply, searching his face as she did so. A second or two passed with nothing said.

"You can't do it, can you?" she screamed. "Fuck you. I'm going home. I may or may not be there when you get there." She stormed off, leaving the service robot and suitcases to collect her belongings.

That could have gone better, Calvin reflected as he walked though the park and recalled the incident. He looked around the park, which seemed to be brimming with happy couples. He noticed them and scowled.

As far as he knew, Bianca and he were still a couple, and slowly working to be a happy one again. Bianca didn't move out and Calvin was able to smooth things over with her, eventually. Unfortunately this temporary truce was predicated on Calvin's agreement to severely limit his time with Tarpa. They weren't to go anywhere secluded like Myst Village anymore, and no more physical contact. Calvin had agreed, and the two of them had made up (as evidenced by the bout of make-up sex they had shortly after). Calvin reflected that make-up sex was great, with that flood of emotional and physical relief that washes over you and your partner as you both re-affirm just how much you mean to each other. He thought that it was a terrible shame that you had to fight first to have make-up sex.

Calvin's display lit up with alerts—an urgent rescue. He ran down the trail to the nearest ODIN station. Approximately a minute later he emerged from a similar station roughly one half kilometer away. He darted down a trail for a few hundred meters and then jumped into the woods while following the translucent arrows that were visible in his display.

He quickly made it to a section of river with some rather unpleasant looking rapids. A man was in the middle of the rushing water and clinging onto a rock. A loop of rope ran around his left arm and also around, and attached to, a yellow overturned raft. The raft was being violently tugged by the rapids. At the other end of the raft, down stream, was a little girl hanging on to the same loop of rope. The man was screaming to her over the noise of the rapids, begging her to climb onto the boat, but the pull of the water was too strong for her. It was evident that she was going to lose her grip soon.

Calvin saw that the only feasible way to rescue her was to go further downstream and wait for her. He quickly ran along the bank to the beginning of another cluster of rocks. He jumped from one to another, working his way to the point where he thought the current was likely to take her.

The last jump he took was a far one. His foot slid as he landed on the wet, moss-covered rock. He landed heavily on his side and the jagged rock cracked a rib. Stunned, he rolled off the rock and into the rapids, which swept him brutally into the side of another rock. Calvin had just enough wits about him to grab onto the rock.

Calvin then heard the screams of the little girl coming near. He turned his head in time to see her glance off of the very same rock that he had slipped on a moment ago. He managed to turn himself around so that his back was to his rock. He knew that the force of the current would keep him pinned in position as long as he stayed centered on the rock face.

He watched the girl as she came closer, scrabbling to stay above water. He cursed when he realized that she was likely going to pass slightly to the right of him and his rock. He lunged against the current, using his feet to push him slightly upstream and to the right to meet the girl. Somehow, he was able grab her by the waist, spin around, and push her up onto the top of a mercifully flat-topped rock.

At this point Sir Issac Newton reminded the world about balancing forces, and so Calvin was now underwater and to the side of the rock, where the current swept him further downstream, over a small four-foot waterfall, and onto the top of another rock where he landed with a hard, wet thud. A moment later, a yellow raft glanced off the side of his head and woke him from borderline unconsciousness.

Calvin slowly and painfully sat up. He grabbed a canteen that he kept in a specially fortified pocket for just such emergencies. It was labeled "Tang+". He gulped it down vigorously. As he drank, he could hear the man, presumably the girl's father, yelling to her to stay where she was.

Calvin stowed the canteen. He couldn't see the father or the daughter, and neither of them could see him because of the waterfall. He cupped his hands and shouted to the two of them, "I'm all right. I'm just over the side of the small fall up ahead. Please, both of you stay exactly where you are. Give me a minute to catch my breath, and I'll be back to get you."

He heard the man yelling back, "OK. Honey, you heard the man. Stay there and don't move." Calvin couldn't hear the girl, if she answered at all.

OK, great, thought Calvin. Now that I've promised them that I'll save them, how the fuck am I supposed to do it? He saw the raft a little ways downstream, stuck on another cluster of small rocks. He noticed the rope that lined it.

He was feeling better—the Tang effect was healing him. The pain killers he had added to the Tang were also working. Thankfully, the current was much more docile at this point in the river. He slid off the rock and back into the water. He floated stomach up, feet first downstream and used his feet to protect him from the upcoming rocks. He climbed onto the rocks and grabbed the raft. He used his augmented strength to whip the raft around and fling it onto the riverbank. At this pointed Newton told him to go jump in a lake, or more accurately, fall into a river.

Calvin was ready for it, though, and swam swiftly to the bank. He grabbed the raft and ran up the bank to the position of the little girl. He set the boat down and gave the rope a quick squirt of liquid nitrogen and then broke it with his hands. He then pulled the rope free from all of its fastening loops except two and then securely tied it to those two loops. This gave him maybe ten meters of slack rope. He tied the other end of the rope around his waist and turned to face the girl.

"I'm going to throw the raft over to you. Don't get in it until I tell you. Do you understand?"

The girl nodded. Calvin was glad to see that she wasn't acting too panicky. However, she kept looking upstream toward her father. She seemed to be more worried about him than herself. He was still in the water, unable to climb up the steep, slick rock that he was clinging to. He was positioned mainly upstream of the rock, but he kept dangerously leaning out into the current to check on the state of his little girl.

Calvin called out to him, "Sir, I'm going to throw the raft over to your little girl in a minute and then we'll come and get you. Are you OK to stay there for a little longer?"

There was a moment of silence and then, "Yeah, I think so. I don't really have a choice, do I?"

Calvin ignored the sarcasm. "Good. Then I want you to move back directly upstream of the rock. Neither I nor your daughter want to see you get swept away in the rapids, and we both need to focus on getting her to safety."

"OK, just save her."

Calvin turned back to the girl. "Hey, sweetie. Look at me. Your Dad is fine. The sooner I can get you, the sooner I can save him. I need you to pay attention to me. I'm throwing the raft now, OK?"

The girl nodded. Calvin spun a few times while holding the raft. He looked like a silly version of an Olympic hammer thrower. He released it and the raft flew out over the river. The wind caught it and it nearly knocked the girl off of her rock. That would have been embarrassing, thought Calvin with a wince.

He pulled the raft back to shore and tried again. This time he aimed further upstream. The raft landed just beyond the girl's rock. As the current brought it closer to her, he pulled the rope so that it would strike directly against the center of the rock. It struck, bounced, and stayed put.

"OK, sweetie, jump into the raft. Jump!"

The little girl crouched, and jumped. Calvin thought her amazingly brave. He quickly pulled her to the bank where she scrambled out of the raft and grabbed Calvin's leg. She looked up at him in panic. "Save my Daddy!"

"OK, don't worry," he said calmly. "Your Daddy is fine."

"No! She screamed. She pointed at the river behind Calvin and screamed again, "Save my Daddy!"

Calvin spun around. "Jesus!" He exclaimed. The father was coming down the river, fighting to stay afloat. Calvin threw the raft again and it landed just in front of the father, moments before he was about to smack into a nasty looking group of rocks. Instead, the man slammed into the raft and grabbed onto one of the rope loops. Calvin pulled the boat, and by extension the man, to the bank and quickly pulled the man out of the river. The man seemed to be largely unhurt, but he looked exhausted. Calvin pulled out a mobile PatientMan from another reinforced pocket. The man's stats soon appeared in Calvin's vision. No broken bones. Good. He was going to be all right. He checked the girl. She was clinging onto her father's chest as he lay on the bank. She was fine too.

Calvin allowed himself a moment to relax. He sat down on the bank a few feet from the other two. He was so tired that he could barely speak, but he made the effort just the same.

"I did a scan. You are both OK. No serious injuries." The father managed to speak through exhaustion and tears of relief. He said, very softly but audibly, "Thank you."

"Calvin nodded to himself and pulled out another flask that he kept for just these types of circumstances. The label on the flask read "Scotch". He took a long hard pull of it.

CHAPTER 34

Catatonic

Bianca and Chuck were walking around the city while continuing to master their new-found ability. Bianca, who had more experience with the ability than Chuck, suggested that they practice the floating viewpoint. She said that Ariel told her that it only works when there are several people or cameras around, because Ariel needed several reference angles to accurately generate a virtual perspective.

They worked out that the best way to do this was to "float" behind themselves as they walked through the city. So here they were, watching themselves from above and behind as they walked around the city. It was sort of like playing a third-person video game. But unlike a video game, they both had to concentrate on walking, which was difficult to do without the feedback from the eyes. They found that in time their other senses—especially the sense of touch, became stronger to compensate for this.

At first they lurched awkwardly around the walkways of the city, but after a while they became skillfully aware of their bodies enough that they soon walked normally and stopped getting worried stares from the other citizens.

They experimented with moving their perspective to the side of them as they walked, but this made them stumble and feel like they wanted to vomit. This was going to take more practice.

Suddenly Bianca stopped and stood dead still. She told Chuck to wait a second. Chuck, now looking through his own eyes, turned around to meet her. She was obviously still not "at home", so to speak, because she stood dead still with her eyes forward and unmoving. She was breathing hard.

"What is it?" asked Chuck.

Bianca murmured, "Give me a second. Something is up with Calvin.

"What's wrong?" he asked.

Bianca, without consciously thinking about how to do it, sent Chuck the same feed that she was watching. His body froze while facing hers, with his eyes also facing straight ahead.

An old couple, who earlier had seen them lurching around the city, made comments about the sorry state of the youth these days and so on and such like. Bianca and Chuck continued to stand like statues, directly in the flow of the walkway. For the most part people just ignored them, apart from the occasional curious stare or two. This was a city after all—if everyone stopped and looked at all the odd things and odd people, no one would ever get to where they were going.

Meanwhile, Bianca and Chuck were watching the feed in rapt attention. It was a live feed from Calvin's display lenses. He was being thrown down rapids like a rag doll. He went over a waterfall and landed heavily on to the rocks below. The two bodies standing in the city cringed simultaneously, causing the people nearby to jump away.

Now the feed was still, showing only the clear blue sky and the rushing water of the waterfall. Chuck came back to his body to talk to Bianca, but she was already gone.

Bianca made her way as quickly as she could to Calvin's location. She kept the upper right-hand quarter of her vision showing the feed from Calvin's perspective. From time to time, during the really intense moments, she would stop suddenly and watch the feed.

By the time she made it to Calvin, she found him sitting on a river bank facing a man who was lying on his back, motionless except for breathing. A little girl was next to the man with her arms draped over him, hugging him. Calvin was taking big swigs from a flask.

Calvin heard someone coming and turned to see who it was. He was expecting another ranger, but saw Bianca running toward him instead. He was too tired to be surprised or to even speak for that matter.

Bianca stopped running a few feet away from him. She walked carefully up to him and hugged him cautiously, knowing that he was likely badly hurt. As she did, she said to Calvin softly, "I love you." Nothing more needed to be said.

She sat down next to him and noticed the writing on the flask. She reached out and took it from his unresisting hand, took a big drink from it, and handed it back to him. The two of them sat peacefully still except for the motion of passing the flask from one to the other. They were there for an unknown period of time, both half catatonic, until more rangers came to help.

Calvin vaguely remembered slaps on the back, a firm handshake from a teary eyed father, hugs and kisses from a little girl. But what he mostly remembered later on were the simple words spoken to him from Bianca—"I love you."

CHAPTER 35

Strawberries

Calvin woke up in his own bed, feeling slightly groggy as always. Calvin was not a morning person. In fact, on some days he wasn't even an early afternoon person. Today, however, he was going to damn well try to be because he and Bianca were going to spend the day together.

Bianca had kindly gone to take a shower first, allowing Calvin some time to get used to being in the vertical position again. While he waited for Bianca to finish her shower, he decided to kill some time by watching his now favorite feed, Evionia.

He never admitted this to anyone, of course. Although he had to assume that Bianca knew and did not care because, well, Bianca knew everything, and if she had a problem with something she was not shy about pointing it out.

This was the one rotten strawberry in the otherwise red and juicy strawberry carton of their relationship. Sometimes when Calvin would get that prickly feeling on the back of his neck that he might have done some laughably innocuous thing that was going to land him in hot water, he would have to remind himself that he loved Bianca and it was worth it.

And he did love her, he knew. But he also knew that he had been reminding himself of that fact more and more frequently these days. And heaven forbid he visited Tarpa, oh my god, you would think that he had just raped a chicken to hear her carry on about it. But he loved her. Oh, yes.

So, feeling that he was fairly safe in doing so, Calvin tuned to a random spot on the planet of Evionia. He watched a farmer plowing a field. The planet's inhabitants were at the early stages of an industrial revolution, but because there was no oil on the planet most machines were powered by distilled alcohol. Unfortunately, so were most of the inhabitants.

This particular farmer was driving up and down the field in a make-shift tractor. However, presumably as a motivational aid, he would allow himself a drink at the end of each row. This meant that the rows started off fairly straight and true, but gradually became more and more wavy the farther one looked down the field. This culminated in the farmer trying to plow a tree stump and flipping his tractor on its side. The farmer was unharmed and, not surprisingly, laughing. He hollered for his two oldest sons to come, and when they did, the three of them tipped the tractor back upright and banged the front wheel into something close to straight.

The farmer then handed the bottle of spirits to the oldest son, smacked him on the back, and told him to "git 'er done".

Calvin thought about this and contrasted it with his own life. Somehow, right now, just messing around and not getting yelled at for it sounded very, very tempting.

And speak of the devil, Bianca came out of the room while toweling off her hair. She was naked, and quite stunning to look at. This reminded Calvin that there were still some very nice strawberries left in the strawberry carton of their relationship. What were some more? Well, she was certainly smart now, that was for sure. And she had a great sense of humor, was very feminine, and generally very loving—unless she got annoyed of course. Then, well, it wasn't funny. Nor was it feminine and certainly not loving. But he loved her. Oh, yes.

"So Cal, have you thought of what you wanted to do today?"

"Yeah, actually, I was thinking we could start with the Big Breast Museum—it's much classier than it sounds."

—STARE—

"I'm kidding, of course," said Calvin with a grin. "How about we go learn how to ride horses?" he asked tentatively.

Bianca looked puzzled and asked, "Horses? What on Earth made you suggest that? Oh, I know, you were watching that hillbilly channel again weren't you?"

"Yeah, maybe that was it—I don't know. I just thought it would be a neat thing to try. Not your cup of tea?"

Bianca shook her head.

"Well," said Calvin, "let me see . . . How about . . . fishing?"

Bianca shook her head again.

Calvin continued, "OK, so you're not into doing outdoorsy things today; I'm feeling that. Perhaps something a bit more cultured. Hmm . . . The Big Breast Museum is cultural but you said no to that . . . hmm . . . How about . . . we try making pottery together?"

Bianca furrowed her brow.

Calvin shook his head. "No, I expect not. Something passive then perhaps? How about . . . we go view some flower gardens together?"

Bianca's eyes lit up.

Calvin smiled. "Yeah, I thought so. I already mapped out a few of them this morning."

Bianca swatted him with a girly slap to the shoulder. "You jerk. You love to wind me up, don't you?"

Calvin shrugged. "And yet you never catch on that I'm not as insensitive and stupid as you make me out to be. One day maybe you'll have a little faith in me."

"Yeah, yeah," replied Bianca with rolling eyes. "So, what places did you pick?"

"Well," answered Calvin, "The first place is The Big Breast Flower Show. Oh my, you should see what they can do with pussy willows." He looked at Bianca expectantly.

She stared back at him blankly and said, "Ha ha ha."

"See!" exclaimed Calvin, "Now you're catching on." He then made a mental note to skip that one. Damn, and he was really looking forward to it.

And so the two of them spent the day milling about the botanical gardens in the area. The gardens were quite breathtaking with attractions such as ornate flower tunnels, bushes pruned in the shapes of cute little creatures, and even some very interesting sculptures sprinkled around to add to the general feeling of artistic tranquility.

It was a perfect day for walking hand-in-hand and sneaking kisses under the shade of a tree. Lunch had been some delicate little something-or-others, very tasty but not entirely filling. They remedied that by filling up on wine.

As they traveled home, Calvin reflected that it was these sorts of days that made it easy to love Bianca. If he could just get her to ease up on the surveillance, and perhaps ease up on how often she was hanging out with Chuck, then everything would be dandy.

Oh yes, Chuck. She was going to play tennis again with him tomorrow, wasn't she? Or whatever it is they do together. Honestly, talk about double standards. And it's not like I can even spy on them with Ariel. Well, I did ask Ariel, didn't I? And Ariel just said everything was OK. I can't imagine Ariel would lie—I'm not even sure she can. But still . . .

The packet they were in arrived in their apartment's garage, which snapped Calvin out of this moment of introspection. Bianca walked through the door to the dining room, followed by Calvin.

Calvin always made sure to stay behind Bianca when entering the house. This was because of the ritual that had now built up between Bianca and Velcro. Every time Bianca would return home, Velcro would run to her at top speed and leap into her arms.

Bianca thought it was terribly cute, although admittedly Velcro had been putting on the pounds and would nearly knock the breath out of Bianca. Still, she didn't have the heart to make him stop.

This time was no exception, and Calvin thought he was going to have to catch Bianca for a moment because the impact even made her take a step backward.

Calvin snickered, "We are going to have to start leaving padding for you in the garage."

Bianca agreed, "Yeah, right, I know. But he's so darn cute," she then rubbed her face on Velcro and continued, "Yes you are, aren't you? You're so cute. Mommy loves you."

Calvin was a little jealous by this. And then he was a little ashamed that he was jealous of a cat. He thought—you're a sad man, Calvin Jones.

CHAPTER 36

Numb

Tarpa was on the beach staring blankly at the ocean. She was trying not to think but merely to exist. She was listening to the crashing of the waves, the whistling of the breeze, and the calling of the seagulls.

Life seemed to be drained of all pleasure for Tarpa. Much of it was now spent right here, on the beach, staring into infinity. This was another new state of being for her, this numbness, this void, this depression. Nothing really mattered much to her anymore, even the fact that nothing mattered to her anymore.

She had been this way ever since Calvin last had dinner with her. Calvin had sat her down and tried all so delicately to explain that Bianca would prefer it if they limited the time that they saw each other to a bare minimum. He told her that it tore his heart out, and that he hoped that, in time, things could go back to normal.

Tarpa was understanding of the situation and did not press the issue with Calvin. She left it up to him to decide when and where they would meet. She hoped, like Calvin, that Bianca would eventually lighten up and she and Calvin could regain their close friendship.

But the longer she waited, the more she started to feel like she was waiting for a day that would never come. So now she spent most of her time trying not to think about it. Of course, this meant that in a perverse sort of way it was the only thing she thought about—a fact that was even starting to show in her work ethic.

Her last "Dark Angel" mission had gone smoothly enough, but the execution lacked any of her signature flare. A man had been sitting at his kitchen table, eating a bowl of cereal. Suddenly, he saw Tarpa walking purposely toward him with a blank expression on her face.

The man exclaimed, "Who are you? How did you get in here?"

Tarpa simply stabbed him in the throat and said, "You suck," and then went home.

CHAPTER 37

Playtime

Bianca and Chuck's activities together had now reached a stage that one might even venture to call epic. Long passed were those clumsy days of getting a face full of beach ball. Long passed, too, were the days of awkward tennis.

No, these were the days of blindfolded mixed martial arts. The days of juggling knives. The days of Kung Fu Frisbee.

Neither of them knew exactly why they were doing this—things just sort of escalated. Certainly this behavior was uncharacteristic of Bianca. In fact, had Calvin seen Bianca during these times with Chuck, he would have probably chalked her up to a doppelganger.

Somehow whenever she was in the presence of Chuck, Calvin's delicate little Bianca would turn into someone that Calvin would probably associate to Sarah Connor, the mother in the *Terminator* movies who protected her son from killer time-traveling robots. Bianca, however, never really put much thought into it. To her, it was still just playtime.

Kung Fu Frisbee was a challenging sport and it also kept the local kids entertained. It was especially popular with a child named Zack, not because he liked to play it but because it meant that the other kids were no longer playing the game "Hide Zack's Shoes". Here is the gist of how it was played:

Bianca and Chuck would stand in the middle of a field, surrounded by dozens of little kids with Frisbees. Bianca and

Chuck would then start sparing, drawing from several different martial art disciplines.

The kids were told that if they hit either of them with a Frisbee, then Chuck and Bianca would take them for ice cream. And so, as the two battled, the kids would randomly throw their Frisbees at them. The kids were always stunned to see one of them turn around in the nick of time and catch the Frisbee even though there was no possible way that they could have seen it coming.

Of course, the children had no way of knowing that their display lenses were actually providing the necessary data that Ariel used to enable Bianca and Chuck to see from any vantage point.

After Bianca or Chuck would catch a Frisbee, they would then throw it back at one of the children. If the child was hit by it without catching it, then they were out. The game ended when all of the children were out. The rare few children that landed a hit were indeed treated to ice cream and the other children had to call them "Ninja Master" for the rest of the day.

CHAPTER 38

Truth

The next couple of months for Calvin were mercifully peaceful, with very little fighting at home or heroics at work. He and Bianca were getting along OK, but not great. Bianca and Chuck were still going on "play dates" as he sarcastically called them, as it seemed they were always playing tennis, playing catch, or playing some other strange little game they made up for the day.

Also, Calvin found himself missing his time with Tarpa. He was getting increasingly agitated that it was taboo to see Tarpa, but Bianca could see Chuck whenever she wanted.

One day, feeling slightly put-off by how happy Bianca seemed after one of her play dates, Calvin finally pressed Bianca on exactly what they were doing together. Bianca saw the irritation flare up in Calvin's eyes when she said that she really could not tell him. In the end, Bianca did finally give in and tell him, not wanting to ruin their relationship over a misunderstanding.

And so she spilled the beans, telling Calvin about the ability that she and Chuck possessed. She recanted the story about the first day they played catch, and about walking in the park from behind themselves, about Kung Fu Frisbee, and even about the time that they got thrown out of a bar when they won too many times at poker.

"Why didn't you tell me sooner?" asked Calvin.

"Chuck asked me not to."

"Why?"

"Because we are pretty sure that it's not legal here. Bob said that you have to ask permission before Ariel will let you look through other people's feeds, but somehow we don't have to."

Calvin considered this. "Who is going to stop you? Who will punish you? Ariel is the law here. She is obviously letting you do it. You two are weirdly intertwined with her now. I imagine you can do it because she can do it. I don't know that it's ethical, but it sure ain't illegal. Not here."

Bianca thought about it. Calvin saw her eyes widen.

"You see it, right?" asked Calvin. "You two are local gods now. You've got all the knowledge of the world ready for your instant retrieval. You can watch virtually anyone, anywhere. I imagine you can control just about anything too, because just about everything in this world is wired into Ariel. For you, the TV just works, the shower just works, and your boyfriend can be under constant 24-hour watch. So, tell me Bee, how's it feel to be a god?"

"I never even thought of it that way, Cal. I swear. I just—it just sort of happened, gradual-like." And then a though struck her, "So, do you feel uncomfortable around me?"

Calvin nodded slowly. "A little. Yes."

Bianca was visibly saddened. "So, what now then?"

Calvin shook his head. "So nothing. Bee, I still love you. It's not like this is new to me. I mean, I pretty much knew that you could watch me. I am, I have to say, jealous of you and Chuck. Not like you think, just jealous of your power. Ariel doesn't even really like me, I'm sure of it. Now you two can do all this stuff. I just worry that one day I'll lose you to Chuck, simply because this thing that you share is so powerful."

"That's silly."

"Is it? I'm not so sure. And then in the mean time, I can hardly even see my friend."

"So it comes back to that?"

"I don't know, Bee. I'm trying to be fair about all this. But when I think about it, I sort of feel I'm being short-changed here."

Bianca was getting a little annoyed at where this was leading. She decided to put an end to it. "You know Cal, it's not like she's really your friend, anyway."

"What do you mean, of course she is."

Bianca shook her head. "Sorry, Cal, but no. I didn't really want to bring this up. I didn't want to hurt you. But I see now that it's better for you to know the truth."

"What truth?"

"That Tarpa is using you as a guinea pig."

"No she's not. What are you talking about?"

And so Bianca brought him to the telescreen and showed him the truth. She showed him video of Tarpa weakening the trunk of a huge oak tree moments before the same tree fell on Calvin. Next, she showed him video of Tarpa deliberately setting fire to the woods—the same woods that nearly burned him alive, but instead ended with yet another tree falling on him. Finally, and irrefutably, she showed Calvin video of Tarpa taking manual control of a combine harvester, steering it toward Calvin, and then jumping out of the cab and into a strawberry patch moments before it tore Calvin's arm off.

Bianca turned to him. "I'm sorry; she's not your friend. She and the gang at Bobcorp3 have been experimenting on you, testing the limits of your healing."

"She . . ." Calvin began. He had no words. Anger and betrayal were having a knock-down, drag-out fight inside of his head. Suddenly, he felt again that he was all alone. His girlfriend was a freak and his only friend kept trying to injure him behind his back. It was just too much to take. He stormed off wordlessly into the garage and took ODIN down to the city. He needed to think.

Bianca thought about running after him, but she decided to do it virtually instead.

Calvin: Tarpa, we need to talk.
Tarpa: OK, what about?
Calvin: Just meet me at Myst Village as soon as you can make it.
Tarpa: Really Calvin? I'm on the West Coast.
Calvin: Yes.

—Pause—

Tarpa: OK. See you in about four hours.

Calvin momentarily felt very bad for suddenly dragging Tarpa across the country with no notice and no explanation. He had only seen Tarpa a few times in the last few months, once to race cars, and twice to have dinner together. Calvin had told her about the situation with Bianca, and she was visibly hurt by it. Still, Tarpa had accepted the situation gracefully. But it was clear that neither of them was happy about the situation and it put quite a large damper on their fun together when they had to pretend not to be too "friendly", or else the wrath of Bianca would come upon Calvin's ass.

Calvin thought to himself, I have to hear it from her. I don't know that I can trust Bianca anymore. Maybe she's making it up. Maybe those videos were just from her imagination. I can't be sure. I have to ask.

Calvin made his way to the edge of the city via ODIN, and then took a car the rest of the way to Myst Village. On his way, he saw a squirrel patiently standing by the side of the road, waiting for him to pass. After Calvin did pass the squirrel, he watched it in his rear-view display. The squirrel looked both ways and then crossed the road. Hmm, thought Calvin, evolution at work—neat.

After arriving at Myst Village, Calvin killed a few hours playing the game until Tarpa showed up. Once she did, he invited her to join him in the game.

Once they were both in the game, which was designed to keep the many players separate from each other by using a combination of deceptive imagery and movable landscape, Calvin took his lenses out. Tarpa took the cue and did the same. They were now reasonably safe from the prying eyes of Ariel, and by default, Bianca.

Calvin then said to Tarpa, "Thanks for coming."

Tarpa shrugged. "You would do it for me. So, what's up? You fighting with Miss Pu . . . with Bianca?"

"I'm not sure. Maybe. It depends."

"What's that mean? Depends on what?"

"On what you tell me next."

"About?"

"About your work at Bobcorp3. Bianca told me that you guys have been doing experiments on me. She showed me video. Video of you setting up the accidents that almost killed me. Is it true? Please, tell me the truth. If you respect me at all, tell me the truth. I'm prepared to believe you either way. For all I know, Bianca is making it up."

Tarpa's two-part brain went into a defensive huddle. There was a discussion of strategy, of subterfuge, of hiding the truth, of telling the truth, weighing the risks and rewards of all possible answers. Somewhere in the discussions a third part of her brain, a new part, some impetuous child named emotions, answered for all of them. Out of some bizarre feeling of loyalty, Tarpa answered, "Yes. It's true, bu . . .."

Calvin backed away. "Oh my God. Get away from me."

Tarpa held up her hands. She said gently, "No, please, wait—let me explain. I'm sorry, Calvin, it's true that I did that to you and it's inexcusable. I know it's no use saying that I was just doing my job, but that's why I started it. And I know it's even worse that I kept doing it because I was angry with you for being with Bianca instead of me. But Calvin, the more I did it, the more I felt awful about it—so much so that I stopped doing it after the incident with the harvester. I was the one who did the surgery on you after that, you know. I saw your limp, nearly lifeless body on the table and I thought to myself, Tarpa you're disgusting.

"I thought about what would have happened if I missed and ran you down with the harvester. I thought about how terribly sad and alone I would be without you. You know I have problems with emotions, Calvin. But I'm pretty sure I felt disgust. I hated myself. And so after the surgery I went to see Bob. I told him I wasn't going to do it anymore. I even got him to agree to abandon further experimentation all together. I'm sorry Calvin, please forgive me. I'm sorry. I'm sorry. I'm sorry."

She was crying. She dropped to the ground, limp. "I'm sorry. I'm sorry. I'm sorry. I'm sorry."

Calvin couldn't take it. He rushed over to her and hugged her. "Shh. It's OK. I forgive you. I really do forgive you. It's OK. I understand."

"I'm sorry. I'm sorry. I'm . . ."

"Shh."

Calvin held her, rocking her gently. He didn't know what to think or do. This was all just too much. He liked her, maybe even loved her in a strange way, but he was hurt by her betrayal. And he was frightened by this breakdown she was having. She seemed practically suicidal. It was so far out of character for her that it made his skin crawl. She seemed to have unraveled. He was very, very unnerved by it.

"I'm sorry. I'm sorry. I'm sorry. I miss you. I miss you. I miss you. I'm sorry. I'm sorry. I love you. I love you. I love you." and then silence.

Now there was another emotion for Calvin to contend with, and even more concern over how to handle Tarpa. He looked at her; she was sad, shaking, and helpless. A mistake now, he knew, could fundamentally alter everything.

He kissed her.

Yes, that's it—a mistake like that.

CHAPTER 39

Influence

Bianca stalked around the apartment, back and forth, back and forth, her anger increasing with every step. How dare he just walk off like that? How dare he? I should have run after him.

And so she restlessly watched Calvin through the Ariel system. It annoyed her that he immediately sent a text to Tarpa. It annoyed her that Tarpa immediately came running to Calvin without thought. It annoyed her that they were trying to meet in secret. It annoyed her that she had to sit here, passively waiting.

She watched, godlike, as Calvin made his way to Myst Village. She watched as Tarpa rushed to get her belongings together. She watched as the two made their separate ways to the meeting spot.

She watched as the two conspirators removed their display lenses, mistakenly thinking that it gave them privacy. She watched and listened as Tarpa apologized. She watched Tarpa as she had a mental breakdown. She watched Calvin as he comforted her. She listened to Tarpa's unending apology, and her declaration of love.

She watched Calvin kiss Tarpa.

She threw up.

She broke things.

She wanted to see Chuck.

Instantly, she was standing in Chuck's apartment.

Chuck was walking from the kitchen to the living room with a cup of tea in his hands. He saw Bianca appear two feet in from of him and dropped his tea.

Bianca said, "Chuck! Chuck. I need to see you."

Chuck shook his head, not to say 'no' but to try to get his head straight. It took him a second to get up to speed. Finally he realized that she was nothing but an Ariel-created hologram, a living dream. She was not really there, but his brain was being made to see her. Finally, he answered, "You scared the shit out of me."

"I'm sorry. I need to see you."

"You're seeing me now, aren't you?"

Bianca could indeed see him. Ariel was an immensely powerful creation with almost limitless memory capacity. She effortlessly tracked not only the actions and positions of the Earth's inhabitants, but nearly every object they came into contact with as well. Because of this, even without multiple cameras, Ariel was able to provide Bianca's brain with a reasonable representation of Chuck and his apartment.

"No, I want to meet for real. I don't know what to do. I fucking hate Calvin. I think I'm going to kill him, and his psycho-bitch lover."

"Lover?"

"They're meeting behind my back. I just saw them kiss."

"Shit, I'm sorry. Listen, don't do anything crazy. Come over here. We'll figure something out."

Bianca nodded. "I'm on my way." She vanished.

Now back in the real world, Bianca began to gather up a few of her things and shove them into her suitcase—she wasn't going to bother taking much. As she did this, she knew she wasn't coming back. She cried as she packed, occasionally cursing Calvin and breaking a few of his things.

Velcro saw that his Mommy was upset and hopped up onto the bed to cheer her up. He saw the open suitcase and jumped in. Bianca threw a couple of shirts on top of him and closed the lid without noticing.

Bianca then set the suitcase to follow her and left for Chuck's place. She opted to walk to his apartment complex on the other side of the city because she needed time to think and time to walk off her rage.

She walked the trails of Newark in a trance-like state as the sun was setting in the distance. She mindlessly bumped into a girl on the trail. The girl, annoyed, said, "Watch where you're going."

Bianca shoved her hard. The girl fell to the ground. Bianca towered over her. "Fuck you. Just die you stupid bitch." She kicked dirt at the girl, who flinched.

Bianca looked around. People were staring at her. She exhaled sharply in annoyance and continued on her way.

At this point in the story, it is important to understand the nature of the Ariel system. Ariel, being a distributed artificial intelligence, was comprised of millions of individual nodes and the interconnections thereof. There was a little part of her in every device that ran her code, most of these being the PCs (Personal Communicators) that virtually every citizen had implanted behind their ears. The PCs, along with display lenses, allowed everyone to access the Ariel system but they also WERE the Ariel system. Every new node added power to the system—more memory, more computing power, and more interconnections between the virtual synapses that formed Ariel's artificial intelligence and creative problem solving abilities.

There was a potential problem with this arrangement, however. Logically, it would take a finite amount of time for all the signals and information to travel from node to node. In much the same way that it probably took several seconds for a large dinosaur to feel pain when something injured an outer extremity, so too could it take hours for Ariel's farthest nodes to communicate with each other. This problem could have left Ariel a slow and ponderous thinker.

To get around this flaw, the Bacons created Ariel with what they called Priority Influence Code. In accordance with this code, decisions whose influence was likely to be local were made with the consensus of just the nodes in the area. Also, events and decisions that had to be acted on quickly were also made with local nodes. Ariel's priority was always to use the most number of nodes that she could manage, given the time restrictions of the situation.

Ariel's "thoughts" and logical decisions were constantly being synced and double checked with all other available nodes. In this manor, a split-second decision could be made, but it could also be corrected or nullified as more and more of her brain processed the information.

This same mechanism was used to prevent the introduction of mutated forms of the Ariel code from infiltrating the system. All outputs of any node were always double-checked against the outputs from other random nodes, both near and far. If a node was found to be acting strangely, it was immediately ignored by all other nodes, effectively disconnecting it from the system.

Because of this novel system, one could say that every person had their very own, slightly unique Ariel system that centered around their own PC. Each of these systems overlapped one another, but the strength of that overlap diminished with distance. But because of the syncing process, everyone's version of Ariel remained more or less the same.

To visualize this, picture a piece of thin rubber that has been loosely stretched over a hula-hoop, or some other similarly-sized frame. Visualize the rubber as sticky. Now, picture several marbles being places randomly around the surface of rubber, with the stickiness keeping them in place. This represents the city of Newark, with each marble a node of the Ariel system. The depressions in the rubber caused by the weight of the marbles represent the sphere of influence each one has in the area. The deeper the depression, the greater the influence. You'll also notice that the depressions diminish as they radiate away from the marbles in the same way that each node's influence fades over distance. Also note that areas with several marbles close together form their own deeper, combined depression.

Now, to visualize the destructive influence that Bianca was exerting on the Ariel system, drop a basketball onto the sheet of rubber.

Bianca's brain, with its trillions of interconnections, absolutely dwarfed even the most advanced PC when it came to the neuro-networked aspect of Ariel. One could say that it is in these interconnections that Ariel's personality exists. Bianca's brain, filled with anger and retribution, was holding sway over virtually all of the other nodes in the city. Without a doubt, in her immediate area, Bianca WAS the Ariel system.

And so it was that Bianca's anger toward the girl had immediately sent the girl's karma deep into the negative and an immediate hit was ordered on the girl. It was tragically unfortunate for the girl that a Dark Angel was nearby and well within Bianca's sphere of influence.

The girl got up and dusted herself off. She continued to walk down the trail when yet another woman bumped into her. This time she thought twice before mouthing off, and merely excused herself. The woman said nothing and continued on. The girl shook her head and walked on also. After a few hundred paces or so, the girl dropped dead of a heart attack.

Bianca, oblivious to all of this, continued her walk to Chuck's apartment.

CHAPTER 40

Disconnect

Scattered around the world, random nodes were being asked to verify the outputs from Bianca's brain. Nodes closest to Newark naturally acted first. Due to the unnaturally large scale of Bianca's "node", the chosen nodes pooled resources from those around them. In many cases, it took the nodal resources of whole cities to replicate the power of Bianca's brain.

One by one, each of these clusters reached the same conclusion: there was a faulty node. The node clusters centered around York and Philadelphia made the discovery first. Together, they vetoed the validity of Bianca's "node" and sent out an "Order to Ignore".

As the order spread its way through the system, other clusters checked the validity of the order but could find no fault.

Within ten minutes from the time of the incident between Bianca and the girl, the "Order to Ignore" permeated back into Newark. Collectively, every node surrounding Bianca suddenly turned their virtual backs on her.

Bianca, who by this time was crying on Chuck's shoulder, grabbed her head, froze, and then collapsed to the floor in a limp puddle.

Chuck, panicked, lifted her onto the couch. She was breathing but unresponsive. Eerily, her eyes were open and unmoving except for the occasional involuntary blink.

He did what he could to make her comfortable. He fussed over her for nearly ten minutes when, suddenly, he too dropped limply to the floor.

CHAPTER 41

Thaw

Deep in the bowls of the K6B Museum, a man sat up from a suspended animation chamber and looked around, blinking. He was in a large, empty room. The back quarter of the room, the quarter in which the man found himself, was sectioned off from the rest of the room by very thick cardion. In the center of his section was his suspended animation chamber, which was diamond-shaped and also built of very thick cardion.

The man's name was Kevin6 Bacon and he was the protector of the Ariel system. Kevin6's life had been a strange one. From the time of his birth Kevin6 worked to complete the Ariel system by writing most of the code that ran the system. When he was around 60 years old and the Ariel system was fully implemented, he agreed to be placed into suspended animation so that he could be called upon by future generations whenever the Ariel system needed tweaking.

Since then, his life had consisted of him waking up in the museum every decade or two to perform some tedious emergency computer work. On some lucky occasions, Ariel would agree to let him take a day or two of vacation from the museum before having to go back to the oblivion of suspended animation. Ariel always advised against it, but Kevin6 would always argue that if he didn't get out and see the world once in a while, he might lose the will to protect it.

He thought about the comedy of these outings. He, a 60 year old man, traveling with an entourage of at least three Dark Angles as body guards. It always put him in mind of Charlie's Angels, a TV show that was ancient even to him. He liked those outings.

Kevin6 stretched and stood up. He walked over to the cardion wall and looked around. Usually there were humans gathered to speak to him, but not today.

He was about to turn away when he saw a lady leading a large tour group into the other side of the room. She started in surprise when she saw him. Flustered, she quickly herded the group back out of the room.

That was odd, he thought. And then he looked down and realized that he still hadn't dressed. Unabashed, he casually dressed and then exited his secure bunker—an action that automatically signaled the guards to remove any tour groups, secure the house, and remain on high alert.

He waited for about five minutes and received the all-clear signal from the leader of the guards. He then walked to the next room over, his den, and sat down at a desk to check on Ariel. He pulled out an "old-fashioned" pair of glasses, dark tinted with stems on them that hooked around his ears. Kevin hadn't really been out much lately, for obvious reasons, and so he had missed the bodymod revolution. The glasses had a small coil of wire on the side with a plug. He plugged it into the PC behind his ear. Wearing them, he resembled a stereotypical secret service agent. Now prepared, he checked in with Ariel.

Interesting, he thought—it appeared that Ariel herself had summoned him this time. This was a very rare occurrence. He read Ariel's report, which detailed Blick's "Ariel Generation project", a project created to turn human minds into organic parts of the Ariel system. He read about Bianca and Chuck. He read about the incident between Bianca and the girl. He read about Ariel's action to disconnect Bianca from the system.

He shook his head in annoyance. "Why can't they leave well enough alone?" He did some more research and then sent an "Order to Ignore" for Chuck. It paid to be cautious. He also contacted Bobford3 and proceeded to rip him a new asshole.

For Bobford3, this was tantamount to being scolded by the ruler of the world. After some "discussion" between Kevin6 and Bobford3, it was "decided" that the Ariel Generation project should be terminated immediately.

With the situation now under control, Kevin6 walked to the kitchen and made himself a sandwich and some tea. He relaxed in his recliner and flipped idly through some old, dusty books while he contemplated what to do next.

CHAPTER 42

Castle

Calvin and Tarpa were still in Myst Village. It was dark now, and they had decided to camp in the village for the night while they took some time to sort out their increasingly complicated lives.

They were in the master bedroom of a simulated medieval castle. It was probably meant for the king of the castle, but they didn't worry because the castle was abandoned.

Calvin was lying on the bed next to Tarpa for warmth. The linen was fresh, so Calvin supposed that the maintainers of the game must have anticipated the occasional sleepover by weary gamers. They were both fully dressed and, surprisingly, had not slept with each other. Tarpa was sleeping shallowly, but Calvin was still awake.

They hadn't spoken much after the kiss, neither one really knew how to take it. Tarpa did say one thing, however, before going to sleep, and it was the main reason why Calvin was still both awake and fretting. What she said was this: "Sooner or later you're going to have to chose, Calvin. You can't have us both."

Calvin wondered in what kind of world a man finds himself choosing between a woman who repeatedly tries to murder him, and one that is a jealous and omnipresent god. He also wondered what kind of man he was for loving them both. The more he thought about it though, the more he felt that he loved Bianca for what she used to be, and he loved Tarpa for what she was becoming. He knew, logically, that his affections were shifting, but emotionally it was still impossible for him to let go of Bianca. He really wished that he could do something to help her—something to turn her back to normal. But then again he knew that if he did take away her powers, she would probably hate him for it.

Some time later he felt the need to use the restroom. When he found it, he was grateful that the creators had made it semi-modern so that he was not going to have to do his business over a smelly hole in the floor. Unfortunately for Calvin, he realized too late that he would have to put his lenses back in to flush the toilet because it was controlled from within the game. He felt at this point that it probably did not make a difference—after all, he knew that Bianca most likely already knew that he and Tarpa were alone together.

Calvin clicked his lenses into place and saw that a message from Ariel was waiting for him. It read:

Ariel: Calvin, because of Bianca and Chuck's brain augmentation, they have been causing irregularities in my functioning. Recently, Bianca caused a sufficiently large irregularity which resulted in a death. This irregularity triggered an automated response that disconnected her from my system. Furthermore, Kevin6 Bacon has been activated in order to handle this situation. He has ordered Bobford3 to cancel any further such experimentation. He has also ordered the disconnection of Chuck from the system. As a consequence of the disconnect, both Bianca and Chuck are now both in a coma. They are both currently located in Chuck's apartment and I am sending people to collect them. I am alerting you of all this because neither Bianca nor Chuck have any living relatives so you are therefore the closest relation to either of them. In the absence of your feedback, I have made the decision to have them sent to Bobcorp3 in the hopes that they can bring them out of their comas or possibly even return them to a state close to normal. I await your reply.

And so Calvin quickly wrote back.

Calvin: Ariel, thank you for everything. Please continue with the plan to bring them to Bobcorp3. Please urge Bobford3 and Blick to undo the modifications ASAP. I will be there directly.

Instantly, a reply appeared.

Ariel: Bianca and Chuck are already on a shuttle to Bobcorp3. I have contacted Bobford3 and he agrees with your wish to return them to normal, but he needs Blick to help with the surgery. Unfortunately, Blick has left the moon 25 minutes ago because he was not happy about his project's cancellation. He will not answer my attempts at contact. I will continue to work toward an amiable conclusion.
Calvin: Thank you. Please keep trying.

Calvin ran back into the bedroom and woke Tarpa. She saw that he was wearing his glasses. She instantly thought about what Bianca might be seeing through his lenses. She panicked and pointed to Calvin's face with a gasp and said, "Calvin—your glasses."

Calvin touched his face. He quickly caught her meaning. "Oh, no, that doesn't matter now."

Calvin then explained to her the situation. After hearing it, Tarpa offered to come with Calvin to the moon, both for moral support and to offer Bobford3 her surgery skills. Calvin was surprised by the gesture and thanked her.

After some debate, they decided to spend the rest of the night in the castle and get an early start the next morning. Just to mess with Calvin, Tarpa stripped down to her underwear before going to bed. Calvin, who in all honesty could have found another bedroom to sleep in, decided on a middle road and climbed into bed with Tarpa—but still wearing his jeans. Tarpa smiled to herself. She knew that it would only take another kiss to get them off of him, but she restrained herself. She was proud of that.

CHAPTER 43

Socks

"**M**r. Bacon, sir. I'm terribly sorry to disturb you, sir. It seems there is a gentleman, I think he said his name was Prick or something like that, well, he's banging on the door and demanding to meet with you—something to do with a canceled project as far as I can tell. Shall I have him removed from the premises?" asked the tour guide with as much professionalism as she could muster.

Kevin6 considered. He could send the man away, but these types of things when left unchecked tended to fester. It wouldn't do for this man to hold a grudge against him. The last thing that he needed was a stalker. No, better to deal with it now.

Kevin6 looked up from his tea and said, "Send him in, please." He thought for a second and added, "Guarded."

"Yes Sir."

A moment later, Blick walked into Kevin6's den flanked by two serious-looking guards. The den was more like an English study. It was the sort of room that one might imagine to be inhabited by a distinguished elderly gentleman who smokes a pipe and drinks brandy by the fireplace. Sadly, there was no fireplace, but everything else was spot on. It was a celebration of all things mahogany and burgundy. Paisley rugs were represented, as were oppressively tall bookshelves.

"Have a seat," prompted Kevin6, gesturing to a seat across from him. In between the two seats was a low table containing a tea set and biscuits.

The man was still standing and looked like he was about to shout. Kevin smoothly interrupted him, never raising his voice. "Please, do have a seat and help yourself to tea and biscuits Mr. Prick."

"It's Blick," snarled the man.

"Fine, yes, of course." Kevin6 cleared his throat. "You see, Mr. Blick, I do not respond to threats and I do not listen to yelling. I do not," he said as he motioned to the guards, "but they do. So please, have some tea and let us see what we have to talk about."

Blick looked at the guards, and then forced a smile. He sat down. Kevin6 poured him some tea and slid the cup over to Blick's side of the table. Blick ignored the tea and grabbed a handful of biscuits instead.

Kevin6 raised an eyebrow at him in silence. He then steepled his fingers and frowned, a gesture known the world over to mean, "Well?"

Blick said in a mockery of politeness, "Look, sir, with all due respect I think you are making a mistake. My project is the future. Man's evolution no longer takes place in his genes, but in his mind. It's our ideas that shape us. We must continue to use our minds, our technology, to improve ourselves. We owe it to the future of mankind to allow projects like mine to proceed. Otherwise we will be left in the evolutionary dust, forever shielded from our technology instead of bettered by it. So please, sir, for the betterment of mankind, will you please let my project continue?"

Kevin6 sat back in his chair and stared up at the ceiling in thought. After a few seconds of this he looked back at Blick and said, "No."

Blick exploded. He made a move to stand but a large, unfriendly hand pushed down on his shoulder and prevented it.

Kevin6 raised a finger and silenced him. He then said, "You make a very good point but you are missing an important detail."

"What's that?" snapped Blick.

"Your project simply will not work. You could never introduce your subjects to the Ariel system without extreme imbalances—we've already seen that. What's more, organics are inherently unstable. It would only be a matter of time before the code was corrupted and the whole system went to hell. No, I am sorry Mr. Blick, but I'm afraid I'm going to have to stand firm on my decision."

Blick considered his options. It didn't seem as though Kevin6 was going to be persuaded. Time for plan B then, he thought. He sighed and contrived to look deflated. "Yes, OK, I suppose you're right. I still think it could work, mind you, but not when a system is already in place. I can see that now. I'm sorry I snapped at you. It's just, well, you know how it is. You put a lot of work into something and you hate to see it all fall apart."

He leaned forward and took the cup of tea from the table and added, "Well, no matter. It's not the end of the world." He leaned back again and casually sipped his tea while kicking off his shoes, making himself at home.

A few seconds later, Kevin6 and the two guards went still. Blick smiled and said to himself, "Hypnotic sweat sock gas. Ha! That guy Drakke was a loon, but I'm sure glad I read through his notes."

Blick quickly walked over beside Kevin6 and whispered in his ear, "I like the Ariel Generation project. I am going to help Blick restore it."

Kevin6 parroted, "I like the Ariel Generation project. I am going to help Blick restore it."

Blick continued to give him suggestions, which ultimately guided Kevin6 to cancel the "Order to Ignore" for both Bianca and Chuck. Kevin6 also crafted a secured and encrypted loophole that ignored any irregularities that the system might otherwise see in Bianca and Chuck.

With that sorted out, Blick suggested that Kevin6 forget about the loophole. He then put his shoes back on, sat back in his chair, and clapped his hands loudly.

The two guards immediately jerked back to attention. Their hands instinctively started to move for their weapons, and then realized there was no threat and stood down. Kevin6, too, looked startled for a moment, then confused, and then calm again.

Kevin6 said apologetically, "I'm sorry, what did you just say? I think I'm dosing off. You would think that I already had enough sleep for a lifetime, huh?"

Blick said, "I'm glad you decided to reconsider the project. I look forward to working with you in the future." He stood up and continued, "Well, it is getting late. I'm sorry to keep you up. Do get some sleep. Oh, before you do, though, could you please contact Bobcorp3 and let them know the good news?"

Kevin6 yawned and replied, "Of course. Thank you for the visit. These gentlemen will show you out." He nodded at the guards.

Blick bowed his head slightly and left with the guards. Kevin6 rubbed his head, and then contacted Bobford3.

Outside, Blick reflected that he was glad that he tried the sock trick out on Calvin first, because Calvin had rambled about Ariel's secret maintenance mode and his failed attempt to hack it. He also rambled about his love for Bianca, his love for Tarpa, his favorite color, that he wanted a pony when he was little, that he had a birthmark on his ass that looked like Elvis, and that he sometimes drooled in his sleep.

CHAPTER 44

Surprise

Calvin and Tarpa were in the elevator at Bobcorp3. No one told them the good news; Bianca wanted it to be a surprise. It was.

As the door opened and the two were about to step out, Bianca and Chuck stepped toward them from opposite sides of the hallway and said in perfect unison, "Oh, hi Calvin. Nice of you to interrupt your honeymoon to visit your comatose girlfriend."

And so, Calvin was indeed surprised—surprised that Bianca was already out of her coma, surprised and creeped out that her and Chuck were talking in unison, and surprised by how fast Tarpa had jerked him backward by the shirt collar and stepped in front of him, blade extended.

Again in unison, "Oh my, isn't she protective all the sudden."

Calvin coughed and rubbed his throat. The tug on his collar had temporarily choked him. He cautiously patted Tarpa's arm, a signal which she acknowledged by withdrawing the blade. Calvin was impressed at her sudden composure. He stepped beside her and said to Bianca, "Could you stop doing that, it's freaking me out."

Bianca and Chuck answered in unison, "Doing what? Oh this?" and then they started taking turns with each word, Bianca, Chuck, Bianca, Chuck, back and forth while keeping the pacing and inflection of the sentence perfect, "Why Calvin?

Does it bother you how close we've become? What's it to you, you have her now?"

Calvin immediately went into default mode (injured innocence). "What do you mean? We were just playing Myst."

In unison again, they answered, "We saw you kiss."

Calvin stammered. "That, that was . . . I mean it didn't . . ."

"You shared a bed," they blasted again in unison.

Calvin, stunned, answered on autopilot, "I wore jeans."

Tarpa interrupted. "It's true, he did. I was there."

Calvin looked at her and said in a hush, "That's not helping." He turned back to Bianca and was about to speak when Bianca cut him off, this time speaking solo.

"Enough Calvin. Forget it. It's over. We're through. I'm with Chuck now."

Calvin turned to Chuck, daring him to smile. Come on, he thought, just a hint of a smirk and I'll hit you so damn hard that even Bobcorp3 won't be able to fix you. But Chuck remained impassive, almost even apologetic looking. Calvin's wrath, with no outlet, came crashing back onto himself. He took a couple of deep breaths. He studied Bianca's face. It was cold and uninviting.

Finally, Calvin said, "I don't know. Maybe this is for the best. Obviously we've been drifting apart. And I hate to say it, but you and Chuck do get along well, with all your little play dates and everything. I'm sorry this happened, Bee, but the truth is you're right—I really do love Tarpa."

Tarpa went into stony silence mode. Chuck too remained impassive. Bianca, who was ready to blast Calvin for making another denial, was currently robbed of something to say. For a second, it looked as if she were going to cry. Then suddenly she snapped, "Fuck you!" and stormed off. Chuck gave Calvin a look that simply said, "Dude," and then walked away after her.

Calvin turned to Tarpa and said, "Well, that went well."

Tarpa replied, "Oh yes, real smooth. So, Zero Calvin, it looks like you didn't have to choose after all. It looks like I'm the winner by default." She looked upset.

To Calvin's credit, he was actually ready for this. He may have been known as Captain Oblivious, but right now he was on high-alert and keener than a shark.

"I don't want you to ever think that," he said tersely. "I was thinking about this all last night—that I was in love with what Bianca used to be, but I was in love with what you are right now. I already chose you. I chose you, but then I learned that Bianca went into a coma and I couldn't very well tell you then because of this very reason. I didn't want you to feel like the winner by default. And now Bianca is OK now—granted she dumped me—but she's OK. I could have fought to get her back. I could have begged. I could have lied. But I didn't. Instead, I chose you again. So please, don't ever think that you were merely a convenient second best. I chose you . . . twice." Calvin went to kiss her.

Tarpa pulled away. "Shit," she said.

"What?" asked Calvin, a little hurt.

"I have to work. I suddenly have three Low Karma targets to take care of. Make that four. What the hell is going on?"

"Where at?"

"The mall."

Suddenly it hit them. They said at the same time, "Bianca!"

Then something, maybe a suitcase, whizzed by them in the hallway.

"What was that?" they asked each other.

Calvin said, "I don't know. I think it meowed."

CHAPTER 45

Idiot

"What the hell, Bob?"

"Oh, Tarpa, good morning to you too. Wait, didn't we already have this conversation before?"

"Yes, well, you didn't fucking listen to me back then and now we are in serious trouble. Who the fuck reconnected those two back into the Ariel system? You aren't seriously going ahead on the Ariel Generation project, are you? Are you fucking mad?"

"Ho, ho—easy girl. Easy. Listen, you're yelling at the wrong man. You have to take it up with the big guy himself, Kevin6. He contacted me late last night and told me that he has thought it over and he thinks that the Ariel Generation project is a good idea."

"And you didn't find that the least bit odd?"

Bobford3 shrugged. "A bit. I mean, not a few hours earlier he did call me a 'brainless fucking Neanderthal' for starting the project. But I figured maybe that was just a knee-jerk reaction."

"You idiot. You do know that Bianca caused the death of a girl on Earth just by wishing it would happen, don't you? Well guess what, you brainless fucking Neanderthal, Bianca's done it again—four times. I just got an order to terminate four targets at the mall. If it were a different Dark Angel here right now, they would be dead already—for no reason. Don't you see? Especially while they are on the moon, those two ARE Ariel. Their brains are controlling the majority of the processing power of the whole system. Bianca's whims are leaking into the

191

system. What's even odder is the system doesn't seem to be rejecting them. Something isn't right here. Where the fuck is Blick?"

Bobford3 said in a more serious tone, "Oh, I wasn't aware of that. That changes everything, doesn't it. Blick? Blick left last night as soon as the project was canceled."

"And now, magically, Kevin6 changes his mind. You didn't see the connection? Really Bob? Really? Damn it Bob, you have horrible judgment when it comes to hiring employees."

Bobford3 looked at her sideways and said, "I'll say."

Tarpa shook her head, muttered, "Idiot," and stalked off in search of Calvin.

She found him in the kitchen. She grabbed him by the arm and dragged him into the bathroom. Calvin thought for a second that maybe he was going to get lucky, but it never panned out. Instead, Tarpa reached over and removed his lenses—hers were already out. She said, "We should be private in here. We have to get out of here. I don't trust those two at all. Something's really wrong with Ariel when they are around. I think Blick might have done something to Kevin6 to get him to mess with Ariel. We need to go. I'm going to find Blick and get him to tell me what is going on. You need to meet with Kevin6 in person and see what he knows. Keep your lenses out as much as you can until you get there. It might help to not follow a direct route, but it's your choice—maybe getting there sooner is a better plan. Contact me as soon as you find something out. I'll do the same."

Calvin had been nodding agreement the whole time. Now he said, "Alright, sounds like a plan. I know you can take care of yourself, but be careful just the same."

"I will." She nodded.

Calvin gave her a hug. "OK, let's head for the shuttle."

Meanwhile, Bobford3 was back in his lab and thinking to himself, "I sure am glad I didn't tell her that I approved the next step of the project, genetic manipulation. If she knew we were going to make those two a breeding pair, I think I'd look like Swiss cheese right now."

CHAPTER 46

Zap

Tarpa found Blick at his house in New Chicago. It was a modest home, tidy, and surprisingly well landscaped. She took notice to none of this as she kicked down the door. She found him in his kitchen, making lunch. He actually had an apron on. It made her laugh, despite herself.

Blick was acting like the typical villain, pretending to be completely unfazed by her sudden forced entry—as if this was all part of his evil plan. She was expecting him to say something to that effect at any moment and then start with the maniacal laughter.

"Ah, Tarpa, I though you might come sooner or later. Would you like a kitten sandwich, I raise them myself?"

"Look, shithead, before you start with the maniacal laughter, just fucking tell me what you did to Kevin6. Why did he suddenly change his mind?"

Blick sighed and waved his hand contemptuously. "Oh that—that's easy. I just went over there and talked to him about it. He's a stern man, but he appreciates genius when he sees it."

Tarpa grabbed him and slammed him against the dock. A frowny-face indicator appeared on its smooth, black surface—indicating a need for repair.

"Don't fuck with me. What did you do to him?"

Before she knew it, Tarpa found herself thrown down onto a table top with her air being choked off. Blick's grasp was iron around her neck. It felt like something important was going to pop at any second. He had one hand around her throat, pushing her down onto the table. The other hand held her right wrist and was forcing it against her own stomach. It was humiliating.

Tarpa's left hand was free, but she wasn't strong enough to push his arm away from her, nor did she have the reach to do much with it offensively.

"Don't threaten me, little girl. What? You think you're the only one in the world with electro-muscular implants? I'm at least five times as strong as you, and twice as quick. Now that my test subjects control the Ariel system, there is no reason why I can't just squeeze the life out of you right now."

Blick continued to monologue for some time about how superior he was, a downfall of your typical super villain.

Meanwhile, Tarpa was furiously flicking through the menu system of her electro-muscular system. Tarpa's system was different from most in that she had two large storage capacitors that allowed her system to give her short bursts of speed and strength. These capacitors were implanted in her ample breasts, because hey, there was plenty of room. Unfortunately for Tarpa, even with the help of the capacitors, she still could not push Blick off of her. She was currently trying to activate an experimental "Super Quick Mode", which overcharged the capacitors and pushed the system to its limits. She chose the option and the following text appeared in her vision:

Bobcorp3: Before entering Super Quick Mode, please enter the following passphrase: "I am a stupid idiot. What I am about to do endangers my life and voids my warranty. I agree not to hold Bobcorp3 responsible for any damages that will occur."

Tarpa cursed Bobford3 as her vision started to turn black along the edges. She scrambled to complete the passphrase.

Both Blick and her were sweating with effort. However, Blick showed no signs of weakening. If anything, he just kept pressing harder and harder.

Finally, the passphrase was entered and the system was charged. "OK, time to kick this motherfucker's ass," thought

Tarpa. But before she could move, Blick leaned down on top of her, probably trying to kiss her as she died. Their chests met, and several thousand volts of electricity arced from one of Tarpa's nipples, across Blick's chest, and into her other nipple. Tarpa screamed with the pain, Blick clutched at his chest and then fell back, dead of a heart attack.

Tarpa gasped for breath. After composing herself she quickly ransacked Blick's home until she found a first aid kit. She applied two burn patched over her singed breasts and cursed Bobford3 again. She swapped her shirt for one of Blick's and then she set about looking for clues inside the house.

CHAPTER 47

Fuck

"**M**r. Bacon, sir. I'm terribly sorry to disturb you, sir. It seems there is a gentleman, I think he said his name was Cow Fin Jones or something like that, well, he's banging on the door and demanding to meet with you—something to do with canceling a project as far as I can tell. Shall I have him removed from the premises?" asked the tour guide.

Kevin6 considered this for a moment. He looked up from his tea and said, "Send him in, please—guarded."

"Yes Sir."

A moment later, Calvin walked into Kevin6's den flanked by two serious-looking guards. Kevin6 held his hands up to his temples. The sudden sense of *déjà vu* made his head spin. He pinched the bridge of his nose and prompted Calvin to sit. He poured Calvin some tea and slid the cup over to him. Calvin added milk and sugar, sniffed it approvingly, and sipped it.

"Mmm, Earl Grey. My favorite."

Kevin6 nodded approvingly. "So, my friend, what do we have to talk about?"

Calvin placed the tea down and leaned forward, suddenly serious. "Did someone visit you last night? A man named Blick?"

"Yes, and what of it?"

Calvin searched his mind, trying to figure out how to put it all into words. Finally he said, "Listen, tell me if any of this is incorrect. Bianca, my ex-girlfriend by the way, has some kind of crazy surgery done to make her into a living part of the Ariel system—Blick's Ariel Generation project. She gets mad at me one day, yesterday, and takes it out on a girl. The girl's karma goes deep into the negative and she is killed within minutes. The Ariel system notices this, and shuts Bianca off. Then you somehow get alerted and woken up. You cancel the Ariel Generation project. Then Blick shows up here and suddenly you reinstate the program. Now my crazy ex-girlfriend and her new boyfriend Chuck—also part of the project—are on the moon and ordering hits on random people in the mall that annoy them. Come to think of it, it wouldn't surprise me if I was on the list as well. So I ask you, what happened to change your mind? Why continue all this madness?"

Kevin6 held his head again. He looked dreamily in front of him and said, "I like the Ariel Generation project. I am going to help Blick restore it."

Calvin clapped his hands in front of Kevin6's face and yelled, "Snap out of it, man! What's wrong with you?"

The two guards instantly flanked Calvin, guns drawn. Calvin held up his hands and said quickly, "It's cool guys, it's cool."

Kevin6 shook his head and regained himself. He motioned to the guards to lower their weapons.

"That prick!" exclaimed Kevin6. "He did something to me. He must have hypnotized me or something. I remember most of it now."

"OK, well, no sense worrying about it now. First, you need to shut those two down again before things get out of control."

Kevin6 said, "Yes, you're right. Give me a moment." He then put on his glasses and jacked them into the PC behind his ear. A moment later he said, "Fuck."

"What's wrong?"

"He, I mean I, put some kind of protection in place that keeps me from shutting them down. The system won't respond to my 'Order to Ignore'. I must have encrypted it, but I don't remember the key. Shit."

"Have you tried the one on the side of your vault?"

Kevin6 looked at him sharply. "What do you know about that? Hey, wait a minute; you're THAT Calvin aren't you? Calvin

Jones—the one that tried to hack into Ariel. I've been meaning to talk to you about that, you stupid . . ."

"Yes, yes. Look, I'm sorry. It won't happen again. It's just a character flaw I have. Whenever I see someplace locked, that's where I want to be. I used to climb out of my crib as an infant. Then, my parents set up a gate, and within a week I figured out how to open it. But look, that's not important right now, is it? Right now we have to stop Bianca and Chuck."

Kevin6 replied, "OK, but we'll talk about this later. For now, yes, we need to talk to Blick. Any ideas about where to find him?"

"Actually, my friend Tarpa went to find him. Let me call her real quick. Excuse me for a second."

Calvin went outside the house for a moment so that he could replace his lenses and use the Ariel system again. Calvin stared at nothing in particular and said, "Hey Sweetie. Any luck with Blick? I'm here with Ke . . ."

"Shh. Shut up. I'll be right there," answered Tarpa cryptically and then hung up.

Calvin shrugged and went back inside.

"She's on her way," he said to Kevin6. "I think she didn't want to talk over the Ariel system."

"Smart girl," answered Kevin6.

The two of them played chess and chatted while waiting for Tarpa. Calvin lost every game. He also got lectured about never, ever interfering with the Ariel system. He took it with as much good humor as he could. Finally Tarpa arrived, escorted by the tour guide.

Kevin6 got up from his chair and said, "Thank you, Gladas, that will be all for now." He turned to the guards and said, "You two can wait outside the door. We need to talk in private and this lady here is one of my most loyal Angels so there is nothing to worry about."

Kevin6 then motioned to his chair and said, "Please, Tarpa, have a seat. Oh, and do not, whatever you do, squeeze the armrests here and here. That will trigger this table to spring with near-lethal force into your friend over there."

Tarpa sat down and smirked. Calvin said, "Don't you dare."

Kevin6 resumed, "OK. Well, Calvin has brought me up to speed. Apparently Blick put me in some kind of trance or hypnosis. He had me install a protection scheme that keeps me from blocking those two as nodes. In order to remove it, I need to know the passphrase from him. Did he tell you anything? Can we talk to him?"

Tarpa went rigid. She tensed up and nearly grabbed the arm rest too tightly. Calvin noticed this and exclaimed, "Let go!"

Tarpa looked at where her hands were and relaxed them. She then mumbled, "He's dead."

They both answered with a variant of, "What was that?"

Tarpa said, louder this time, "I said he's dead, alright. I'm sorry. It was an accident."

"An accident," ranted Calvin. "What, you accidentally stabbed him in the head?"

"No!"

"What then?"

"I don't want to talk about it, OK." She looked sheepishly down and added, "It's embarrassing." For some odd reason she cupped her breasts.

Calvin, distracted by the gesture, let it go at that. He then said to the room in general, "OK, so now what do we do? Anyone?"

Kevin6 was biting his nails. He looked at Calvin and asked, "You said that Bianca was your ex-girlfriend, right?"

Calvin answered cautiously, "Yes . . . so?"

Kevin6 paced back and forth a time or two. Finally, he said, "Well, there is a way out of all this."

"What?" asked Tarpa and Calvin together.

Kevin6 looked from one to the other and back again. Then he said, "We have to kill them. It's the only logical way out. If we can't disconnect the nodes, we have to shut them down manually, so to speak. I'm sorry."

Calvin shook his head. "No, there has to be another way. Listen, Bianca is my ex-girlfriend but that doesn't mean I want to see her dead. There has to be some other way? Can't we do something else? Fix her brain or something?"

"Calvin," said Kevin6 kindly, "I'm sorry. Blick is dead. Who can do the surgery now? Even if we could, how would we catch those two?"

Calvin thought for a moment and asked, "For that matter, how would we kill them? I mean, they know just about everything that's going on. How do we battle that?"

Tarpa, who was already working the puzzle in her head, answered this one. "Don't worry about Chuck, I can get him. I know a way. But Calvin, I'm afraid you will have to take care of Bianca."

"Why me?" he asked instinctively without thinking about it.

"Because if I killed her, a part of you would resent me for it. I don't want that between us. Also, because I think the best way to get her is for you to win her back as a girlfriend, reestablish her trust, and then do what you have to do."

Calvin shook his head. "I don't know if I can. Let me think about it."

Tarpa went over to Calvin and put her hand on his shoulder. "It's OK. I understand. But listen, we probably don't have much time before all this gets away from us."

Calvin nodded but said nothing.

Tarpa then excused herself, saying she was going out to do some reconnaissance and would contact them in an hour or two.

"So wait a minute," began Kevin6, finally putting two and two together, "don't tell me that Tarpa is your new girlfriend."

Calvin nodded. "I'm not sure it's official yet, but yes."

Kevin6 was astonished. "Son, you sure know how to pick them, don't you? Bianca and Tarpa. A rogue node and a Dark Angel. Some day, when all this calms down, you're going to have to explain how that happened. I didn't even think Angels were wired like that. Isn't it a bit like dating a robot?"

Calvin shook his head. "No, not really. OK, a bit, but she's not like she used to be. She's actually very pleasant."

"Pleasant!" exclaimed Kevin6, choking on his tea. "Calvin, she is one of my most lethal Angels. I mean, this one time I sent her to take care of this . . ." He trailed off as he looked at Calvin. "You know what, you probably don't want to know. I couldn't eat for days after it, I'll tell you that. But, hey, whatever works for you. Just don't ever, ever make her unhappy—that's my advice."

Calving forced a laugh. "Yeah, I know, I know. I'll be careful. But I'm telling you, she's different now."

Their conversation was broken by Tarpa stomping back into the room and screaming, "That bitch! I'll fucking gut her like a pig and make her eat her own intestines!"

Calvin turned to Kevin6 and said, "That isn't to say she doesn't still have her moods."

Calvin then asked Tarpa, "What's wrong? I thought you were going to go do some surveillance?"

"Yeah, well, as soon as I put on my lenses I was sent a Low Karma warning from Ariel. And that bitch Bianca sent me a text that read 'Ha Ha Ha. Now you are a target too!'" Tarpa was steaming. She turned to Kevin6 and asked, "Can you do something about that, at least? I can't work if I have a team of Dark Angels after me."

Kevin6 replied, "I should be able to. Give me a second." He did his thing with the glasses again and set to work. A moment later he tore out the plug and yanked the glasses off in annoyance.

"It's no good," he said. "Every time I change your karma, it resets back to seriously negative. By the way, he added, you aren't even supposed to know that this is possible, so if you ever use this knowledge or tell anyone about it, I'll do things to the two of you that will make even Tarpa here say, 'Whoa! Hey now, isn't that a bit excessive?' Got it?"

The two of them nodded.

"Good. Now the way I see it, there is only one reason that I can't do this now."

Calvin suddenly stiffened. "I know why," he said, worried, "It's because Bianca and Chuck are somewhere close."

Kevin6 nodded in agreement and then walked briskly to the door of the room, opened it, and barked to the two guards that were standing watch, "Full lockdown, now!" The guards sprang into action.

Tarpa said, "I don't see what all the fuss is about. This makes it easy. We'll take them out now. Well, I doubt you'll be able to use the sneak attack on Miss Pukey now, though, eh Calvin? I mean, you're charming and all, but I think she's after blood this time. Still, we have guards, and we have me. No worries."

Calvin argued, "No, listen, those two are coming as a hit squad and they are coming for us personally. They have near complete control of Ariel wherever they go. They probably have unlimited karma too, since they are such valuable assets to the system. That means they could be coming at us with anything—whatever tools, equipment, or weapons they want. Anything in the world. And instant knowledge on how to use it all. And they've been doing these games together, learning how to cooperate, building teamwork and coordination, training in the martial arts, and even doing creepy shit like looking through each other's eyes. Plus, neither of us can use our modifications because they activate through the Ariel system. We need to take this seriously and we need to be prepared."

Calvin turned to Kevin6 with sudden authority. "Kevin, you go back behind your cardion wall. You have to be safe above all else. If you have to, dive inside the vault as well."

He then turned to Tarpa and said, "Tarpa, you bring the guards up to speed on the situation. Work out the best way to defend this place."

"And you?" she asked.

"I'm going to stay here and pace back and fourth and try not to wee in my pants."

CHAPTER 48

Showdown

If you took the sound of a nail being scratched along a chalkboard, mixed it with the screech of a cat being stepped on, and then amplified the result to about fifty times as loud, then you would make your neighbors very, very unhappy. You would also have a fairly accurate reproduction of the noise that Tarpa, Calvin, and Kevin6 were hearing. The entire house resonated to the sound, amplifying it, destroying any notion of audio communication at a distance.

Tarpa went upstairs to take a look. From out of the window she could see Bianca and Chuck, both of which were holding saws and were slowly cutting through the side of the house. They wore masks and ear plugs to protect them from the dust and noise.

Tarpa darted back downstairs to confer with Calvin. They huddled together in order to hear each other.

Tarpa said, "They're cutting through the wall of the house. I think this whole place is reinforced with cardion. They must be using cardion-tipped blades. It could take them a half hour to cut through. What should we do? I don't think they are dumb enough to just come in through the hole—they'll probably throw some sort of gas or percussion grenade in first. The way I see it, we can either fall back and let them enter, or concentrate fire at the hole, or block the hole before they get all the way through, or just rush outside and gut them where they stand. I vote for gutting, but what do you think?"

Calvin thought about it. "You know, I hate to say it, but I almost agree with you. This would at least keep them further from Kevin6. But then again, we would have almost no cover. I think our best bet is to rig a flap over the hole that they are making—something that will spring shut when we pull a string. If we time it right, we can deflect whatever they throw through the hole back at them. Failing that, we'll fight inside. We'll let the guards take point. We'll wait down here as a second line of defense."

Tarpa shook her head. "I don't like it. Too complicated. How about I just go out there and gut them?"

"Not a good idea," Calvin argued. "They have the advantage. They control the Ariel system. The controls to your electro-muscular implants and arm-knife work through Ariel. Same with my mods too. They would surly block us from even turning them on. Worse, the second we tried, they could take control of our bodies through the system. We have to fight with our own strength, with whatever advantage we can muster. I know that your skin is toughened but you still aren't immortal, and they probably have guns. But, you see, they would be daft to use guns in here—the ricochets could go anywhere. Kevin6 has some good knives in the kitchen. I suggest that we arm ourselves."

Tarpa thought about this. "OK, we'll do it your way. But just so you know . . ." she pressed a spot on her right arm and her arm-knife bolted into possible ". . . I still have my weapon. But riddle me this: why do the guards have guns if they can't shoot inside?"

Calvin shrugged. "I don't know. Maybe they have a special kind of gun. Maybe since they have armor they don't care about ricochets. Maybe they are just crazy. I don't know. Oh, and for the record, I still have my sprayer too. Manual override, eh? Great minds think alike. Anyway, let's get going."

"OK, let's go."

Calvin nodded and they went their separate ways to prepare. Calvin worked with a guard to rig a deflector over the access hole that was being cut. Tarpa collected anything in the house that looked pointy or sharp.

Tarpa and Calvin then met in the hall and waited, peering around the corner. The suspense and the noise of the saw was grating on their nerves. Tarpa turned to Calvin and said, "Look, don't be offended by this, but stay behind me. I know you are tough, but you aren't a fighter and you aren't reinforced like me. If things get really bad, I want you to go behind the cardion wall with Kevin6."

Calvin frowned. "Yeah, OK, whatever."

"I mean it, Zero."

Calvin sighed. "Yes Dear."

Tarpa gave him the eyeball and then went back to watching for intruders.

Finally, the sawing stopped and there was a kicking sound against the wall. The section of wall suddenly broke free and Calvin yanked a string. A table top flapped over the hole just in time to deflect two grenades. A few seconds later there was a terrible explosion outside that shook the house, and then a sudden silence that was only filled with the ringing in everyone's ears.

"Did we get them?" questioned Calvin.

In answer, the table top suddenly exploded into thousands of shards and knocked out one of the guards. Two more objects came through the hole, this time unhampered.

Tarpa grabbed Calvin and said, "I'd say no. Let's fall back. It's going to get juicy in here real soon.

The gas grenades popped and fogged the room. The guards already had masks on and switched to ultra-violet vision to cut through the fog. A shape went sailing through the hole and the guards quickly tracked it and gunned it down. Bullets ricocheted of the walls like very lethal popcorn in a pot. Before the guards realized that this was a dummy, Bianca and Chuck were already inside. The guards fired at them as they looked for cover, but the intruders had shields made from cardion that easily deflected the bullets. It looked like this might have to go hand-to-hand, but the guards out numbered them two to one.

Calvin and Tarpa sat in Kevin6's den, sipping tea. They had secured the door to Kevin6's vault room, but they did not bother to close the door that led to the rest of the house. They had agreed that listening to the sound of that saw again would be a fate worse than death.

"So," Calvin said as nonchalantly as he could, "you doing anything tonight? I was thinking maybe go for some Thai, then perhaps go back to my place and see what happens."

Tarpa laughed. "Yeah, that sounds nice."

They both looked around the room, trying to find something to focus their minds on. Occasionally they would here a muffled scream or a thud, and Calvin would wince.

"Got another one," Tarpa said engagingly. "Only one left now."

"Yep," agreed Calvin.

—SCREAM—

—THUD—

They got up together, dusted themselves off, and stretched.

Calvin said, "I guess it's time to go to work then," and he almost even said it without his voice cracking.

"Yep," agreed Tarpa.

A voice, no, two voices in unison sang out from upstairs. "Come out, come out wherever you are."

Calvin turned to Tarpa and said, "You know when I said we could go back to my place and see what happens? Well, I was talking about having sex. I just thought I should be clear about that—seeing as we are probably going to get killed and all."

"I know, Calvin," hissed Tarpa. "Now shut up and let me concentrate."

"OK, so, just to be clear then, that's a yes, right?"

"Calvin!"

"OK—shutting up."

The attackers sidled through the door with their backs facing each other. They were taking advantage of their shared vision, each one using a section of their vision to watch what the other was seeing. Back-to-back like this they both had a full view of the room.

The two attackers appeared to be unarmed. They wore clothing that was probably bulletproof, much of it covered in blood. Neither one had helmets on. Presumably they were damaged in the fight with the guards, or too stained with blood to see through.

Bianca said casually, "Hello Cal. Hello psycho-bitch."

Neither one answered.

"Oh, OK," said Bianca, "I guess no one's in the mood for chit-chat. Very well."

The two attackers moved instantly and in perfect sync, flanking the room. Tarpa went straight for Chuck. Calvin was farther inside the room, still frozen in place. Bianca was walking very deliberately toward him.

Calvin involuntarily started to back away. He shouldn't be frightened of Bianca, he told himself, but she was covered in blood and had hatred in her eyes. He risked a look over at Tarpa. Her and Chuck were already fighting. Tarpa had two kitchen knives and looked like she was a fighter in a martial-arts style video game. Chuck was just as good, blocking or dodging every single swing. He even landed a kick to Tarpa's midsection, knocking her backward.

He turned back to Bianca, who was still walking toward him very much the way a cheetah stalks a gazelle. He backed up some more and fell into Kevin6's chair. He glanced back to Tarpa's fight. They were getting closer to Calvin's position but still too far for Calvin to worry about. Calvin thought briefly about helping Tarpa, but he knew that as soon as he turned his back on Bianca he would be toast. Besides, Tarpa looked like she might be gaining the advantage. Her attack-style had changed, suddenly becoming erratic and unpredictable. Chucks style was molded from the strict discipline of mixed martial arts. His form was impeccable. Tarpa's style looked like the same way a character in a fighting-style video game looks like when someone panics and starts violently pressing any and every button as fast as they can. Whatever she was doing, it was working. She landed a stab to his chest, but the armor deflected it. Still, the force of the blow actually pushed him back. Calvin wondered how strong she was even without her mods.

He snapped his attention back to Bianca. He motioned to the other chair. "You look thirsty, dear. How about some tea? It's Earl Grey."

Bianca kept coming in silence.

"Stay where you are," Calvin bellowed. I don't want to hurt you."

Bianca stopped, snickered, and kept on walking.

Calvin was seriously thinking it might be a good time for plan B. He glanced back at the door behind him.

Bianca said, "You think you can make it to the door before I can get to you? You wanna try it?"

Fuck, thought Calvin.

Bianca was now at the table. Calvin looked past her. Tarpa had Chuck in a strangle hold. Instantly and precisely, Bianca grabbed the tea tray, spun, and flicked it with all her strength. Before Calvin could even react, the tray hit Tarpa hard on the side of the head. Tarpa lost her grip and stumbled backward. Chuck went back on the offensive. The fighting continued and the two of them started getting closer to Calvin and Bianca.

Calvin finally got his wits and resolved to fight. He went to stand up but Bianca was already in front of him and pushed him back into the chair. Suddenly his world exploded in a rage of fists and claws. He defended as best as he could, but there was no keeping up. He tried to strike back but every time he did it was deflected and it left him open to more abuse. Stupidly, he didn't even have a weapon.

He could hear the other two fighting very nearby. Tarpa was getting tired and looked as if she were loosing again. Chuck kicked her hard and she flew into the other chair, trapping her. Chuck was now fighting very much the same way as Bianca. Tarpa could not get free of him.

Calvin heard Tarpa yell out, "Squeeze the arms!"

The adrenaline of the moment made Calvin's mind sharp. He knew exactly what she wanted because he had wanted to use the same trick on Bianca. He quickly moved his hands to the arms of the chair. Bianca took the opportunity to choke him. Calvin squeezed the arms while Bianca squeezed his neck.

Tarpa saw this and activated her arm-knife, steadying it just in front of her. The table behind Chuck erupted toward his back at near light speed. It plowed into Chuck, forcing him into Tarpa and her arm-knife. The knife pierced his heart as the two of them and the chair all went flying backwards.

Bianca flinched backward and gasped. She must have seen the whole thing from Chuck's perspective. His feed had probably gone dark the instant he died.

Calvin had just enough time to aim his arm at Bianca and cover her with liquid nitrogen. She stood up and tried to bringer her arms up to defend herself but was frozen solid before she could even complete the motion. Calvin exhausted his supply on her, stopping her, quite literally, cold.

He sat there and panted for a moment. Bianca was standing in front of him with a vapor cloud surrounding her. Her arms were in front of her and she looked almost as if she were going to catch something, or possibly hold a baby. Calvin thought she almost looked maternal, well, except for being covered with the blood of several guards.

He carefully extricated himself from the chair, trying hard not to disturb Bianca, and hurried over to check on Tarpa.

Tarpa was just fine. In fact, she was standing over Chuck's body and giving it a good kicking.

Calvin said, "I guess I'm taking you boot shopping again tomorrow."

Tarpa stopped kicking and looked at her boots. They were covered in blood. She smiled.

"Come on," said Calvin, "let's give Kevin the news." He gestured toward Bianca. "I've frozen Bianca. I guess she'll keep for now. We'll probably want to tie her up or something, just in case. I was thinking that we could take her to the moon and put her back into suspended animation. Maybe that would give Bobford3 some time to go through Blick's notes and see if he can undo her surgery."

They unlocked Kevin6's vault room and stepped inside. Kevin6 was still behind the cardion wall. He was sitting at a control center that must have folded out from the wall.

Calvin gave Kevin6 the thumbs up. Kevin6 nodded back and then opened the door to his protective wall. As he stepped out, he said, "Wow, you guys were awesome! That was some team work—I didn't even have to use the lasers or the trap doors!"

There was a moment of awkward silence.

Finally, Tarpa said, "You had lasers?" in a tone of voice that Calvin found surprisingly polite under the circumstances. And polite under these circumstances included anything short of yelling.

Kevin6 nodded seriously. "Oh yes, of course. You don't think I'm going to sit in here, trapped, with no way to protect myself—do you? In fact, we could have all stayed in here and I could have just detonated the whole house if I wanted to."

Calvin was again astonished at Tarpa's composure. She said, "And why didn't we do that?"

Kevin6 looked shocked. "Are you serious? My book collection alone is irreplaceable."

Tarpa and Calvin were covered in blood—much of it their own. They were tired, hungry, and absolutely in no mood for humor. They walked toward Kevin6 with menace in their eyes.

Kevin6 got the hint. He raised his hands up defensively and quickly said, "Sorry. My fault. Honestly, I thought the guards would have stopped them. I didn't use the lasers because those guys were too damn fast."

Calvin said, "Bianca was just walking."

Kevin6 rounded on him. "Oh, my mistake. Are you in fact saying I should have lased your ex-girlfriend? It's not too late you know." He pointed back at the controls. "The controls are right over there. Here, let me just take care of that for you."

"Enough," said Calvin sternly, "I get the point." He glanced at Bianca and then asked Kevin6, "Do you think you could reset our karma now?"

Kevin6 agreed. He worked for a few minutes and was able to reset not only Calvin and Tarpa's karma, but also that of all the other victims of Bianca and Chuck's wrath.

Kevin6 then treated Tarpa's wounds and gave Calvin some Tang—he could heal himself. After that, Calvin and Kevin6 put on insulated gloves and very, very carefully carried Bianca upstairs and placed her near the front door. Kevin6 sent a message to have some people come and take her to Bobcorp3. In the mean time, Bianca stood in the foyer like some kind of dime store Indian.

Tarpa came upstairs to join the others. Kevin6 shook both of their hands in turn and told them that he was forever in their debt. He then looked around conspiratorially and said quietly, "Between you and me, I gave you guys enough karma to retire from work and still live very, very comfortably for the rest of your lives."

Calvin said, "I don't know what to say . . ." but he was interrupted by something tapping at the door. They all looked at each other. Kevin6 peeked out of the window and said, "It's someone's luggage." He shrugged and opened the door.

Bianca's luggage rolled through the door. Calvin recognized it and said, "Hey, that's Bianca's."

The luggage meowed.

Calvin and Kevin6 looked at each other. Kevin6 said, "I think you better open it."

Calvin sent the luggage the command. It opened and a bedraggled cat hopped out. It stretched.

Calvin said, "Velcro, what are you doing here?"

Velcro looked up and saw Calvin. Then he saw Bianca standing behind him with outstretched arms. He ran as fast as he could and leapt into her arms. Bianca's frozen body rocked backward slightly. Velcro's tiny brain instantly registered the extreme cold and ordered his body to jump away. As he did, he pushed Bianca's body over its tipping point.

Time did that slow motion thing for Calvin. It seemed like it took Bianca several minutes to fall, but all the while his body seemed slow and unresponsive. He only made it halfway to Bianca before she hit the ground and fractured into pieces, exposing much of her insides.

Calvin instantly turned away and wretched.

CHAPTER 49

Afterward

It took a few months for things in Calvin's life to return to normal, if that word could ever apply to his new life in the future. Bobcorp3 could do nothing to repair the extensive damage done to Bianca. Even if the Tang effect could repair her body, which was questionable, it was discovered that the back of her skull had also been shattered, along with the memory-related portion of her brain. In the end, Calvin made the hard call to "pull the plug" so to speak. She and Chuck were cremated together and their ashes were scattered into the Pacific Ocean along the same stretch of beach where they all had hung out for the first time.

Tarpa continued to work at Bobcorp3 and at her second job as well. Calvin too, decided to keep working because he really could not think of what else to do with his time and he actually rather enjoyed helping people.

As one might imagine, their relationship went cold for a period after Bianca's death. Calvin had to work through the loss, and Tarpa was respectful of that.

However, Tarpa never let them get too distant from each other and she worked to rebuild the closeness that they once had, little by little, by doing simple things like having dinner together, watching Calvin's silly old movies, and—yes—they even managed to finish their game at Myst Village.

In fact, it was during the end of that game when they finally fell in love. It had been a particularly tough quest. They sat there panting on the steps of a fortress that they had just destroyed, bringing down an evil empire in the process.

Calvin wiped some dust off of Tarpa's cheek. They looked at each other and something in their brains just went 'click'. They both smiled at each other and finally had the kiss that they both subconsciously wanted for a very long time.

The kiss escalated into something more, and the two conquerors made out frantically while the rubble burned romantically behind them.

Shortly after, Calvin received the following text from Ariel:

Ariel: **Congratulations Calvin—you have beaten insurmountable odds. You are now the most appropriate mate for Tarpa.**

Calvin laughed.
Tarpa asked, "What?"
"I think Ariel just gave me her blessing."

CHAPTER 50

Moving

Shortly after their romantic encounter, Calvin moved into Tarpa's house on the West Coast. He quickly found another patch of city to patrol, this time along the San Francisco Bay.

Calvin and Tarpa found themselves to be surprisingly compatible. A major factor in this compatibility was the fact that neither one was a needy person. They both enjoyed the time that they spent together, but either one could also find ways of occupying their time on their own. Because they were both (what some people might call) selfish individuals, this mutual independence worked out very well for them.

Also, neither of them was a morning person, so that was a plus.

Velcro and Astro also formed a relationship of sorts, but this one was not born of equality or mutual respect. No, this relationship was one of dominance and submission, and Velcro ruled it with an iron paw.

The humans, of course, totally misunderstood the relationship and thought it was terribly cute how Astro would let Velcro ride around on his back and steer him around by swatting one of Astro's ears or the other. They also found it cute that Astro would share his food with Velcro, and even let Velcro sleep on top of him on chilly days.

Velcro did, however, kick the habit of running up to people that he liked and jumping into their arms—Tarpa's natural instincts saw to that. This is because the few times that Velcro tried it with her, Tarpa dodged out of the way. After bouncing off of a door a few times instead of landing in Tarpa's loving embrace, Velcro eventually got the hint.

CHAPTER 51

Vacation

One morning, quite unexpectedly, Calvin awoke feeling both happy and alert—it was a totally alien feeling for him.

Things between he and Tarpa were very good. When they were together, Tarpa was surprisingly affectionate and loving toward him. Whether this was born of her emotions or precisely calculated logic, Calvin didn't know and felt that, frankly, with Tarpa it was splitting hairs either way.

And Tarpa herself seemed quite happy. A careful observer might have even called her cheerful—although probably not to her face.

The two of them were able to read each other very well. Tarpa could read Calvin like a book because Calvin let every little thought and emotion play across his face. He had the exact opposite of a poker face. Calvin, in turn, was excellent at knowing what Tarpa was thinking because she would just come out and tell him, a kindness that no other girl had ever shown him. For someone who once had the nickname of Captain Oblivious, this was a blessing beyond compare.

Even their sex life was exceptional. Although sex with Tarpa was always very, shall we say, energetic. So much so that Calvin took to keeping a bottle of Tang+ in the nightstand drawer for use afterward to heal the scratches on his back and the occasional dislocated joint.

Indeed, everything in Calvin's life was going very, very well. But something at the back of his mind was bothering him. Maybe, just maybe things were a little bit too routine these days.

Calvin was pondering this as went out to the kitchen.

"Good stinking morning to you, sweetie," burbled Calvin as he shuffled into the kitchen in his dressing gown and sat down at the island.

Tarpa slid some breakfast over to him and said, "OK . . . what do you want?"

"That's just it," he said, "I don't want anything. I think for the first time in my life I am completely and utterly happy. I have a great job, I have a great girlfriend who even cooks me breakfast (granted it's only instant oatmeal but there is always room for improvement), and we live in this wonderful plastic house together. What else can a man want?"

Tarpa, who knew Calvin better than he knew himself, replied, "You're bored, aren't you?"

Calvin gave a half shrug, "Eh, a little bit if I'm honest."

Tarpa asked, "Did you have something in mind?"

Calvin grabbed her hands and said, "As a matter of fact, I do. I was thinking about a vacation."

"OK, where to?"

"Well, it's very rural and kind of lawless."

"OK, I'm intrigued. Tell me more."

"Well, the people there are really crazy, usually drunk, and here is the best part: there are so many stupid people for you to kill that you may never want to come back to Earth again."

"Back to Earth? Where is this place?"

"Have you ever heard of the planet of Evionia? Well, I was thinking, hey, why don't we go there and bring them the Ariel system? They could certainly use some guidance, and it would give us something new to do."

Tarpa thought about this a moment. Finally she asked, "How many stupid people are we talking here?"

"Thousands," answered Calvin. "Maybe a million."

"OK, I'm in."